HER BIKER'S BITE

M L WINTERS

THRASHER
PUBLISHING

Copyright © 2020 M L Winters
Published by Thrasher Publishing

Second Edition

First edition published 2020 in Romance with a Bite boxset
Second edition published 2020 by Thrasher Publishing
Written by M L Winters
Edited by Carolyn Depew
Cover design by Lana Pecherczyk
Paperback: 978-0-6487777-0-0
Kindle: 978-0-6480188-9-6
ePub: 978-0-6487777-1-7

A Cataloguing-in-Publication record of this book is available from the National Library of Australia.

HER BIKER'S BITE

PRAISE FOR HER BIKER'S BITE

"Her Biker's Bite is a hot ride in more ways than one! Intriguing and sizzlingly sexy, this is a vampire story with a twist, and an ending that will have a lot of readers coming back for more."

— KYLIE GRIFFIN, NATIONAL BESTSELLING AUTHOR OF THE LIGHT BLADE SERIES

"A witty, fast paced, panty-melting story that left me breathless and begging for more!"

— CASSIE LAELYN, AWARD-WINNING AUTHOR OF THE FALLEN GUARDIANS SERIES

"Loved the twists in this story!"

— ANNE D, AMAZON TOP 500 REVIEWER

"An unexpected twist to vampire lore makes for an interesting read and provides a power-packed happy ending."

— HELEN W, GOODREADS REVIEWER

A WORD FROM THE AUTHOR

Welcome inside my sometimes frightening, always romantic mind.

Her Biker's Bite is the first of what I hope will be many stories written by my alter ego, M L Winters. It's the first story in my *Steamy Bites* series and it marks the onset of my journey into the wonderful world of vampires.

I've loved losing myself in the paranormal realm, and I look forward to exploring love with the myriad of characters blanketed in its ranks.

That said....

Thank you for choosing to read Tiff and Gideon's story.

I hope you enjoy it!

Michelle Somers
(writing as **M L Winters**)

DEDICATION

To the four beautiful men in my life—Danny, Josh, Nathan & Gabriel.
Your joy is my inspiration and your love gives me wings.

TIFFANY

*Y*ou should slide into an orgasm like hot fudge sauce slides over chocolate cake.

I tried to imagine that same fudge sauce sliding down my body as a lithe, talented mouth feasted on the dessert, on me. My head slammed the headboard and my eyes shot open.

An earnest, try-too-hard expression filled my vision, the accompanying puppy dog eyes and short-cropped, black curls not nearly as sexy as they were before the onset of our horizontal mambo.

Getting off shouldn't be this hard—pun one-hundred percent intended.

I scrunched my eyes as the heavens opened up outside and raindrops rattled the windows. I tried to lose myself in the moment. In Peter—or was it Paul's—fumbling. His spasmodic *oh, God* and *awwwesome* interjections. The careful groping, the measured, timed-perfect pump and grind, and grunts of him losing himself while nothing came to me. No stars or universe exploding. No thoughts of

England. And definitely no orgasm, earth-shattering or otherwise.

Did I put the wash in before I left?

A vision of my full-to-overflowing laundry basket overtook the image of Peter/Paul's blood-infused face.

Damn, I don't think I did. My work shirt would never dry before morning. That means a complete change of wardrobe for our strategy meeting scheduled first thing.

"Oweee!" Peter/Paul's heavy mass stiffened, shuddered, then slumped against my still wanting body.

My ears rang. My skin pricked sticky with his sweat. His heavy breath prickled my throat.

"Awesome." His hand brushed my breast in practiced, circular strokes. "Hey, you didn't come. Want me to go down and finish you off?"

I shuddered. *God, no.*

He slid down my body, misreading my reaction, which had nothing to do with anticipation. The last guy who endeavored to "finish me off" bit me so badly I couldn't pee without pain for weeks.

I pulled him back up. "Next time."

I tried to smile. Failed abysmally, from the look on his face. That hopeful, eager to please puppy-dog expression vanished, a look that had seen me relent and follow him to his place for a "night cap."

Should there even be a next time? Why did I keep trying, keep hoping that "this time" things would be different? Casual sex, hot office sex, sex with a stranger, sex with a friend. I'd tried it all, with high hopes, only to be left with low—or like now—no result.

No one got me going like Sammy. Always charged, always ready, and as sexy as my imagination. All I had to do was keep him forever supplied with batteries. He did the rest.

In all my experience—not as much vast as varied—men just didn't have the wherewithal—or technique—to get me off. Sammy was reliable and hit the spot. Always.

Did men even know there was a spot? A mere seven letters into the alphabet. Not so far that you'd get lost on the way.

If only I could meet a real-life Sammy, my life would be complete.

"I can't leave you hanging. Let me finish you off."

Hell, back to Peter. Paul? Or maybe Patrick. He hadn't even started. I was already finished. I had laundry to do. And a real bad headache, starting in my temple and finishing smack between my thighs.

I pulled back and glanced at the time.

"Damn, is it midnight already?" I wriggled and rolled till I'd freed myself from his weight. "I have an early morning meeting and a heap of prep I haven't even started yet."

I eyed my silk blouse, folded meticulously on a large chair, along with my meticulously folded A-line skirt. Even my underwear was symmetrically folded in a pile of its own. Foreplay had been as exciting as a wet blanket. No mad rush to get my clothes off and get dirty.

Everything *meticulously* in its place.

That should have been my warning right there.

I slipped into my shirt and shimmied into my skirt. My undies and bra, I stuffed into my bag.

"Thanks so much for—" What could I say? Fun? A good time? It wasn't even mediocre. "Thanks."

I bolted through the door and out into the night, pushing back thoughts of the recent double disappearance two blocks over. Instead, I looked up at the sky. *Please let the rain be gone.* Drops the size of gooseberries began the process of frizzing my hair before drizzling down my back. I ducked my head.

Another hope dashed.

Forever the optimist. Forever disappointed. That was me.

The meeting dragged. It seemed to be the flavor of my life at the moment. Time dragging. Dissatisfaction slumping like uncast clay in the pit of my stomach. Or maybe it was lower.

It didn't help that the new scientist in the newly launched Biological Standards wing of our little pharmaceutical company was late. It made me pissy. Even more so that Graeme—our normally "lateness is tardiness is disrespectfulness" boss—seemed quite blasé about the totally blatant display of tardiness and lack of respect. Welcome to a century when only the semblance of equality existed. The whole bro-code, sexist bullshit still ran rampant in New Orleans, and in particular, in our offices.

The conference room door swung open, and our frazzled-looking—or was that dazzled-looking—admin assistant, Jane, hobbled into the room. Normally she would have stumbled, but hard to do that—or maybe not in the case of Jane—when your leg's still in a knee-high cast. Distraction and the wrong kind of guy could do that to you.

I shoved at the thought, and the telltale pain it brought with it.

Distraction wasn't all bad. Kinda like the guy who followed her into the room.

Jane stuttered, her face so pink she resembled a grapefruit. The pink kind. "Gideon Fang."

Lady parts that hadn't been properly fed in a while suddenly perked up and took notice.

Shit-hot.

No other way to describe the black-leather and denim covered, muscle-clad hunk who strode into the room like he owned it, and every one of us with it.

Nu-uh.

An alpha male with an over-developed sense of importance was the last thing our company needed. My temper prickled. That explained the flow of lava straight through my center—not the motorcycle helmet in his hand or the vision of his thick, muscle-bound thighs wrapped tight round his vibrating machine. Heat burned my face, no doubt to the shade of overripe raspberries.

They'd go down a treat with that hot fudge sauce.

Stop it!

I licked my lips, and green-almost-golden eyes latched onto them. I felt their caress, as if his tongue joined mine in its quest.

Fuck.

That word dragged rampant images to my mind. Inappropriate images for strategy meetings with a room full of stuffy scientists. All stuffy but one.

"Ahh, Gideon." Graeme stood and pumped the man's hand like they were long lost friends.

I hated that I noticed how large and strong that hand looked clasped in Graeme's pudgy one. Hated that my mind flew to the promises a large hand suggested.

"Take a seat. We've only just started."

No indication the meeting had droned for the past half hour, waiting for Lord Gideon to arrive.

I was pissy. Unusually so. I should have ridden Sammy last night, instead of tossing my clothes into the wash before falling exhausted into bed. That would have taken the edge off whatever reaction was taking place right now.

Gideon, our newest testosterone-rich addition to the team, made his way round the table.

Crap.

How did I not notice the only vacant spot sat to my right?

He sprawled into the chair, but not before dropping his helmet onto the table and shaking hands with Mannie—our communicable diseases, or CDC, head scientist—before turning to me to do the same.

I blame my impeccable manners and pitiful lack of balls for letting him take my hand in a firm, pussy-drenching shake. His gaze drilled into mine. Drilled deep, where gazes shouldn't delve.

I snatched my hand free and nodded my greeting. Hard to speak when your tongue's lodged halfway down your throat.

"Now that Gideon's here, let's get started." As if we hadn't started already. Again, my mercury shot skyward. I was over this whole male domination thing. Had been over it since I'd applied for the new role only to be told the company was bringing someone in.

Call me shallow, but my instant dislike—yeah, that explained my reaction—had reason. Gideon had not only usurped the promotion I'd worked my butt off to earn, but he'd also upped the male to female ratio, and it wasn't in double-X chromosome's favor.

"So, as I was saying, work on the Influenza A H3N2v4 antidote has been ramped up, with the new, earlier release date now set for . . . *blah blah blah*." It wasn't like I hadn't heard it all before. I zoned. Tried not to notice the heat emanating from the body beside me. Or the fact his knee bumped mine every time he moved. Which seemed like an awful lot, if you were counting. Which I wasn't.

An hour later, the meeting was over. Just as frigging well. My thighs had aced a better workout than they ever did in yoga. If I'd clenched them any tighter, my butt cheeks would have shattered.

I jumped out of my seat and was at the door before anyone else had risen. Sanctuary, at last. And an opportunity to strategy-plan my avoidance of Gideon in the future.

"Ahh, Tiffany, one moment please." Pudgy finger raised in a "wait right there" gesture, my boss had spoken. And one never ignored the boss. Even when one was so horny, even a look—*not* Graeme's—would turn my already melting body to sauce.

Why did my thoughts always come back to sauce?

And there was another unfortunate word. *Come.* Something I hadn't done in the last twenty-four hours. And curse the fact that if I had, this whole sordid day would have gone a lot differently.

Men didn't spark this kind—or strength—of reaction in me. Never had. No doubt, they never would. Sure, the knowledge never stopped me from trying—hence, my non-event last night—but nothing ever changed. For my sanity, if nothing else, I needed to accept my fate, marry Sammy and move on.

Because whatever reaction Gideon triggered, he was off limits. Regardless of my no work-fucking policy, I didn't do alphas. Been there, done that, and the bruises had healed, just not the scars.

I pushed the memory aside, along with the lump it brought to my throat. "Yes, Graeme."

"I've got an appointment with the Pax Group in the city, so would you mind showing Gideon around?" He turned to the hulk in question. "Tiffany's been acting in your role for the past three months, so if you have any questions, I'm sure she'll be more than happy to help you out."

Then my devoid-of-a-clue boss hand-pumped Gideon once again, before promising to catch up first thing in the morning.

And there sealed my fate.

No escape. No time to take the edge off my craving—even without Sammy. No nothing but eyes that sent me fifty shades of randy and a palm at my back that made me want it to scooch lower.

If this day's end saw me still sane, it'd be one fucking great miracle.

2

GIDEON

Fuck me.

When Damon sent me into Hagen Pharmaceuticals to carry out the coven's plan, I'd never imagined I would be awarded fringe benefits galore, deliciously wrapped in a skittish, tight package with blonde curls and bright, opal blue-green eyes. I could feel her heat. Fuck, I could smell it. And it made me want to taste her like I'd never wanted to taste a woman before. Or, almost never, bar once.

I'd almost lost hope. Surely, she couldn't be . . .

Shock ricocheted through my body, followed closely by a rush that saw every muscle tighten. I'd been wrong before, and the cost was far too great for me to make the same mistake again. That said, the past didn't preclude me from enjoying the feast before me.

Her prim, curve-hugging ankle-length skirt didn't fool me. She was sex on legs, and I couldn't wait to be wrapped in both, hot and tight.

"First, let's check out your office." She gave me, then the

helmet under my arm, such a stern, disapproving look, I was almost fooled into thinking she didn't feel it too. Almost, but for the tiny shiver beneath my palm as I guided her out through the door.

She jerked forward, breaking the connection. "The new Biological Standards wing is down the main corridor and through the double doors at the end." The sharp click-clack of her heels dragged my gaze lower to find slim ankles and firm calves disappearing beneath the slit of her skirt. "If ever you get lost, just follow the olive green tiles. The other corridors have blue."

"I never get lost."

"I'm sure you don't." Her expression said she doubted my confidence, but she didn't bite.

That thought had me hard in less than a nanosecond. I wanted her bite. Wanted to return the favor. My mouth watered, wanting to taste her skin, to pierce it, to savor the delights throbbing just beneath it.

She pushed through the double doors, and even though her retort was stilted and controlled, she left the door to slam in my face. If she expected anything other than a grin as reaction, she'd be disappointed. I pushed on through and followed the sway of her ass.

"So, Tiffany, is it? Or do you prefer Tiff?"

"Only friends call me Tiff."

"Then, Tiff it is."

She glanced back, icicles in her expression. "Tiffany will do just fine." A white building with black trim loomed up before us. "Here we are." Another set of double doors that didn't slam in my face this time. I was fast, just one of my many talents.

A stout, weasel-faced woman looked up from a desk to the left of the entrance.

"Brenda." Tiff's relief was tangible. "The new BS scientist." She turned back to me, focusing somewhere in the vicinity of my right ear. "Brenda, meet Gideon. Gideon, meet Brenda."

She side-stepped when I reached past to shake Brenda's hand, leaving a trail of vanilla and spice and all things wicked. My taste buds sprung to life with the accelerated pulse of her blood and I steeled my jaw against my reaction.

Her smile was tight, lips she'd licked earlier once again receiving attention from her tongue. "I'll leave you in Brenda's capable hands."

She was almost at the door when I intercepted her. "If I'm not mistaken, Graeme entrusted you to show me around."

I was close now. Closer than she'd let me venture before, and her scent was beguiling. Not just the spicy vanilla that made me think of rich, cinnamon-laced cream, but it was her. A slight turn of my head and her throat was within reach— that live, pulsing point where neck meets shoulder stamped with a rosy, half-heart birthmark.

The breath caught in my throat, the world spinning wildly for just one moment. I was all too familiar with broken hearts.

My initial reaction hadn't lied. *She's the one.*

She shuffled back, removing her scent from my nostrils, but not the memory.

"Brenda knows as much as I do about the role, maybe even more. And for anything she can't help with, call me or email." She gave me a once-over and my dick twitched, her only acknowledgement of my very obvious reaction a slight widening of her eyes. And a dusky pink sweeping her cheeks.

I cupped her elbow and was rewarded with a shudder—hers and mine. "I have a question."

She dropped her arm, breaking contact and a connection surely she could feel. Her gaze met mine. *Almost.* She was avoiding eye-contact, and that was fine. Soon that would change, along with her prickly, porcupine demeanor.

It was written, after all.

She quirked a slim, blonde brow.

I didn't make her wait. "Why didn't you apply for the job if you were already doing it?"

Her expression turned to vinegar. "I did."

"Then why didn't you get it?"

"That's a question you'll have to ask Graeme." Her palm flattened against the glass and she pushed, making way for a gust of cool winter air to enter. "Welcome to Hagen Pharmaceuticals, Gideon."

She stalked out through the door, leaving it to slam in my face once again. I let it, enjoying the wriggle of her ass in that tight, sexy skirt. A skirt perfect for pulling up over her hips before pounding into her, watching her derision transform into desire.

Throat-clearing to my left dragged my gaze away from Tiff—yes, she was Tiff to me. One day soon, she'd beg me to call her that, and more.

"Brenda." The thrum-thrum of the old woman's pulse drew my gaze to her neck, to the life-force racing through her veins. I had that effect on women. Now, yesteryear, since three-hundred plus years and counting. But this woman didn't heat my blood, didn't raise my libido. Only one woman had ever held that kind of power over me before today. I'd thought her the match the ancient ones promised. The match to end my restless centuries of yearning and give my unsatisfied soul peace.

I'd been wrong.

And for the two-hundred years since, I'd all but given up on ever finding my match. But now . . . Tiff posed a challenge. And perhaps the promise of more.

I was always up for a challenge. The tight stretch of denim against my cock afforded more than enough evidence of the fact. I let my hand drop, allowing my helmet to shelter my reaction from the other woman's view.

I smiled. "I hear you're an expert when it comes to running this lab. We're going to make a great team."

The woman all but swooned.

It wasn't Brenda who made my grin widen or adrenalin race through my blood. It was Tiff and the knowledge of what she represented. The Prophesy would soon be complete and my existence would be forever transformed.

3

TIFFANY

O ne week.

The longest week in the history of horny women. *Ever.*

Gideon. That name sent both shivers and shudders through my body in one foul and fabulous sweep. Even Sammy had given me no joy, and worse still, no orgasm. A first.

Every time I closed my eyes and let myself go, the face staring down at me was *his*. Eyes of the devil, hot and hungry. Eyes that would eat me up if only I let them. And that was just his eyes. Don't get me started on that mouth.

Sinuous heat hit my core. If I hadn't been sitting at my bench staring vacantly at a line of yet to be swabbed petri dishes, I'd have slithered to the floor in a simpering, pathetic puddle.

I'd relegated Sammy to the back of my underwear drawer until I could separate his mechanical powers from the magnetic powers of he-who-shall-not-be-named.

Damn.

The man wasn't leaving my thoughts—or my dreams— anytime soon. Something had to be done. Maybe an exorcism? Sure he wasn't a ghost, but by hell, he was a demon.

All week, seven long, limitless days of the man. Wherever I moved, there was Gideon. Wherever I turned, his eyes latched to mine, gobbling me up as if they had a tongue and teeth and taste buds of their own.

In the break room, he'd snuck up and reached around me for a cup, the deep rumble of his voice shivering up my spine. In our weekly planning meeting, he'd nabbed the seat beside me before I could find a better option. Even Mannie, with his garlic breath and overpowering sweaty socks, would have been preferable. The stench I could block out, the sense of Gideon's body wasn't so easy. Even in the specimen freezer, the least sexiest of places, he'd edged past to grab the *Staph epidermidis* and I'd nearly combusted with heat.

I was still combusting.

I couldn't concentrate, and my empty, unprepared petri dishes bore testament to that.

There had to be a way out of his spell and back into the real world. One where I didn't lust after the type of man with power enough to destroy the life I'd rebuilt post-Richard.

A familiar clamp wrapped round my chest and squeezed. I'd left that life behind, but that didn't mean it had left me. I focused on the radio, the news report, anything to drag the past from my mind.

Another disappearance in the French Quarter, this time an accountant in his mid-forties.

"So, I was just wondering . . ." Cool breath fanned my

hair and I couldn't suppress the shiver all the way to the tips of my tightly curled toes.

Richard and all his darkness faded into light.

Gideon didn't finish. He leaned in, his cool body sparking heat in my blood, his magnetism pulling at my lady parts until they ached for release, damn them.

Nine days since I'd orgasmed—*yes*, I'd counted—and he damn near had me coming from the mere feel of his presence. I was losing my mind, and all sense of myself. Because, God help me, I wanted to jump the bastard and have him every which way on the spotless lab floor.

I wanted messy sex. Untamed sex. Hard and heavy sex, until I couldn't stand straight or think straight or even fuck straight.

He needed to go before my mind was forever lost. That meant I needed to turn and hear him out. One week, and I knew him well enough to know that only then would he leave.

I braced and swiveled in my chair.

Fuck.

He was so frigging close, barely a flea's dick separated us.

I leaned back and let my gaze slowly ride up his body, trying desperately not to give in to his pull. When it finally locked with those eyes—more green than gold today—I made sure nothing but boredom filled my expression.

I quirked a brow. "You were *wondering* . . . "

"Mmmm."

"Anything in particular, or were you just exercising your vocal cords?"

"Funny, Tiff."

Funny, my ass.

Of course, I didn't say it, much as the words pricked my lips and I longed to put his smart, denim-clad ass in its place. He was determined to wind me up. And blast the man, now I needed a new nickname. One he couldn't ruin, like he'd ruined Tiff. One syllable, and it flowed from his tongue like thick, sinuous honey. Honey that would drizzle down my body till his talented tongue laved every drop of it up.

Fuckola.

This was the worst time for that particular fantasy to hit.

I swallowed, and leaned back as far as my chair and the counter behind me allowed.

Yep, another nickname. Problem was, not much you could do with Tiffany. *Fanny?* That ship was never sailing, no matter how much his using Tiff pissed me off.

"Does your presence here have a point?" My glare was designed to make him feel every icicle-laced dagger. "You're interrupting my flow."

His glance at my still untouched petri dishes said it all. Lucky for him, he didn't comment. My knee was in convenient striking distance of his crown jewels and I wasn't afraid to use it.

"Brenda is off tomorrow, but I have five antibiotics to sterility test. I wondered if you're free to assist."

Fuck, no.

Only I couldn't say that. Fucking workplace etiquette.

"I have a report due by five tomorrow. I doubt I'll have time."

Much better.

"No problem." His lips slipped into a grin that reached all the way between my thighs, and squeezed. "Scratch my back and I'll scratch yours."

Was he trying to kill me? Because no matter how I

reworked those words, they sounded anything but work-related.

This conversation was way past over. I swiveled round and reached for a petri dish.

He swiveled me back, his hand reaching across to stop said dish from skittering to the floor. His arm brushed my breast and neurons shot my nipples straight from erect to mountainous. "I need your help, Tiff. And I'm willing to reciprocate the offer."

Double entendres flowed way too easily from his tongue. Or was it my mind?

I straightened my thoughts, gave them a stern warning and refocused on work. Gideon's wasn't an unreasonable request, really. I'd helped Joel out plenty before he moved cities and transferred to company headquarters. It was the reason I'd stepped so easily into his shoes after he was gone.

Only Gideon wasn't Joel, and the sterility room was the size of a slightly large closet. Sure, we'd be suited up. But we'd be alone and boxed into close proximity for the better part of two hours. Shoulder to shoulder, working side by side. Did I mention alone?

"C'mon Tiff, I really need you for this. Unless there's something else stopping you?"

His last words were a challenge. I felt it, in his tone, in the prick of his gaze. Silence filled with his unuttered words —*you can't handle the heat*.

No way would he get the better of me. I'd help, I'd be professional, and I'd be damned immune to his magnetism.

I grabbed the vial of *E.coli* and shook. "What time do you need me?"

I barely listened as he answered. My mind had turned to defensive action.

18

Sammy was coming out of hiding tonight, because damn everything, I wasn't going into that room with Gideon still unsatisfied.

4

GIDEON

I'd designed the whole "scratch my back" scenario to make Tiff uncomfortable. And, *success*—it seemed to be working. But no way could her discomfort match the dig of my fly against my cock.

Backfire.

Even though the sterility suit—more like a surgeon's scrubs than a hazmat get-up—covered all but her eyes, I could still see her dilated pupils behind the protective goggles, could still catch the heady aroma of vanilla and spice, could still feel the heat of her body as if it were plastered hard against mine.

I'd waited two-hundred-plus years, you'd think I could hold out a little longer. My cock had other ideas.

Five samples, and only the last remained. Her hands were steady as a surgeon's, her eyes directed anywhere but my way.

"Earth to Gideon."

My gaze snapped up to meet hers and missed. She seemed to find great interest in the wall left of my head.

She raised the open Tetracycline tube for me to swab the end. "You're a million miles away."

She couldn't be more wrong. I was right here, with her, mentally doing things that wouldn't keep the tiny sterility room sterile for long.

I swallowed that thought and swabbed. "Yep. On a beach in Bermuda." Her stifled laugh showed the ice was thawing. Slowly. Just way too slow for my liking.

"That's your dream vacation?" I could hear the smile in her voice. It warmed me like Bermuda never had.

A side glance revealed her gaze had now fixed on my hand, but that smile meant I was making progress. And progress, any kind, was good. "I'm not sure it constitutes a dream, but the island has sea, sand and surf—isn't that everyone's idea of a vacation?" I opened the first of five petri dishes and zig-zagged the swab lightly across its surface. "What's yours?"

I held my breath, waiting to see if she'd bite. Just over one week since we'd met, and she was still a staunchly closed book. Deliberately so. No idle chit-chat or personal anecdotes. Just work.

"Skiing in Switzerland."

I didn't have to hide my smile. The suit did it for me. "You like the cold?"

"I like the snow. I wouldn't complain if it was warmer, though."

"There are days in the Austrian Alps where temperatures can range somewhere in the fifties and there's a perfect blanket of freshly fallen snow."

"You've skied in Austria?"

I nodded. "Many times. France and Switzerland, too."

This time she looked at me. Not a limb or an ear. Or even a wall. *Me.* "What was it like?"

If my blood hadn't run cold, I would have warmed from that look. "The slopes in Europe aren't like the slopes here. They're rugged and wild, and virtually never-ending. Some, you start skiing and an hour later you're not yet at the bottom. Of course, it takes an age to walk back up again."

"You walked? Why not ride the gondola?"

Damn.

I'd forgotten myself. Something that never happened, not since the early days. I was practiced in the art of deception. Three hundred years of secrets did that to a man. And for my kind, we had more reason than most to bury those secrets deep beneath a veneer of normalcy. One slip, and a stake through our unbeating heart would mark the end.

No coupling, no soul, no true life. My heart would never know what it is to beat.

One day Tiff would know who I was. Now wasn't the time.

"Sometimes we walk, when we ski off-piste. You get the best runs that way, but the good stuff always comes at a price."

Always.

I took a clean swab and she raised the tube for the last time, oblivious to my blunder. "It's a dream of mine. To ski the Val d'Isère, like my mother did at my age."

Her voice broke, and she replaced the cap this time with more force than she'd used before. "That's it, then." A chill edged her words, the warmth and candor of moments ago gone.

I cut the tip off the cotton bud and dropped it into the vial in her hand. She replaced the lid and averted her eyes once again. "Clean-up time, then I'll leave you to it." Subtext, *sharing time over*.

Just when we'd begun to connect.

Her remark hung between us, frosty, final.

She busied herself with clearing the samples, stacking the swabbed petri dishes in the two-way cupboard. I packed away the trash and passed it to her, before grabbing the gauze and alcohol to begin cleaning, starting with the low ceiling above the built-in counter. Despite her squared shoulders and unswerving determination to stay as far from me as a box-sized room allowed, we worked well together. As if we'd done so a million times before.

We were in sync, just as destiny dictated.

Ethanol vapor filled the room, and I knew she'd be feeling the effects. She exited the room and I cleaned the last of the floor, backing out into the tiny dressing room on my hands and knees before closing the door. I flicked the switch for the sterility room's UV lights.

Tiff stood in the far corner, as far from me as a room measuring three feet by three feet allowed. She'd already removed her hood and had both arms twisted halfway round her back in some weird contortionist move to unfasten the zipper.

I stood back and watched, removing my own gloves, hood and goggles. "Need a hand?"

She barely paused, huffing out her answer. "Nope. I'm good."

I dropped onto the narrow wooden bench and watched a little more. No way was she getting that zipper down without help. The suits were designed with nothing less than impracticality in mind. I wasn't even trying to undo mine.

I leaned back, stretched my legs out to the opposite wall

and grinned. "When you're done, I'll need a hand with mine." I waved her back, even though she seemed determined to ignore me. "No rush."

A few more failed attempts, then she huffed again and dropped her hands. "Fine! You do it."

"Sure." I stood and moved towards her. "Since you asked so nicely."

One frosty glare my way, then she turned, lifting golden-glowing curls to expose the delicate curve of her neck. I leaned in, inhaling her sweet scent and the delights that thrummed beneath. My fingertips brushed her soft white skin as I tugged at the zipper tab. She stiffened.

I could smell her fear, the accelerated rush of her blood, the arousal surging between her thighs. Slowly, softly, I tugged the tab down and inhaled, deep.

My nostrils flared. My cock swelled. My fangs descended, sliding over my bottom lip.

The suit gaped open to reveal a pale blue tee and leggings. Thin. Tight. Tempting. I could feel her heat, her quivering skin. Her need, surging out and calling to mine.

I ducked and ran my tongue across her throbbing pulse. Testing. Tasting. She shuddered. Leaned back. Tilted her head and gave me the permission I needed for more.

I needed her. Now. But our destiny couldn't be rushed. The Prophesy was ancient and finicky, and only those who adhered closely to its dictates could be saved.

I pressed my throbbing cock into her luscious ass and her hand reached back, cupping and squeezing. I groaned, dropping my forehead into her shoulder, praying for fortitude to gods who'd all but failed me in the past.

If I'd had a heart, it would have thrummed with renewed vigor and life.

After two hundred years of hell, I'd finally found heaven.

5

TIFFANY

I wanted it all. His mouth on my throat, his tongue on my breasts, his cock buried deep inside me until we were so tightly joined we couldn't tell one another apart.

It had been too long.

Hah! Who was I kidding? I'd never felt this . . . *this heat*. This fire. This so goddam, fucking good.

I reached back and squeezed the butt that had taunted me since the day his denim-clad ass entered our lab. He pressed his cock deeper between my butt cheeks, groaning into my neck. The vibrations slipped under my skin and rode a lusty trail all the way to my wet, throbbing pussy.

There was too much fabric between us. The zipper was only halfway down my back and I struggled to slip the sleeves off my arms.

A clatter from outside the room snapped through the haze drenching my brain.

Fuck!

I snatched my hands back.

"Stop!"

His hand stalled, but he didn't remove it from where it curved at my waist. "Stop what?"

I wanted to step away, to leave his tantalizing touch behind—cool, yet it burned. But even without the restrictions of our tiny enclosure, my shaking legs refused to function. "That thing you're doing."

'Unzipping you?"

He was, but it had nothing to do with the suit. I was unraveling so fast, my head was spinning.

"I don't like it." The words tumbled from my mouth even while my body still thrummed with everything I'd wanted him to do. Still wanted, truth be damned. Only I didn't want it. *Him.* I couldn't. Not if I was to retain the scraps of sanity and safety I'd built up over the past three years.

"That's not what your body's saying." His fingertips brushed the hair from my neck and skimmed the racing pulse at my throat. "Here."

Cool breath ruffled my hair as his fingers slid downward, beneath the suit, beneath my tee, and slowly, sluggishly circled my breast. "Or here."

His tongue taunted and tasted the racing pulse at my throat as his fingers skimmed out over my ribs, lower. Lower. *Lower.* Until his large, expert hand cupped my pulsing mound and squeezed. "Or here."

I forgot to breathe. Forgot how.

I almost leaned back, almost forgot myself once again.

Another clatter brought me to my senses.

"No!" I wrenched my body away. As far as I could in the square box of a room. "I don't do this."

"*This* being . . ?"

"Sex. At work. With colleagues. With *you*."

He raised a brow, all cocky and self-assured. "Me? Why *me* specifically?"

Visions of Richard rose up before me. Sneering, taunting visions. His thin, bloodless lips spitting out that I was the problem, I was the reason he hated and hit and lost control. That if I dared find someone else, eventually the same spiral would occur, because that's what girls like me drew out of a man.

Nausea surged up my throat and I fought to swallow it back down. "That's not your concern." My palms burned with the cut of my nails, my hands fisted so tightly the pain seeped up my arms. "Just know that this," I unfurled a hand and waved it back and forth between us, "this will never happen again. *Ever*."

I wrenched the door open and bolted. It was well into the lunch hour and whoever had made the noise that brought me to my senses—perhaps Brenda—was no longer around.

Lucky me.

I fled the building and sought the sanctuary of the restroom. I flipped the toilet lid closed and sank down, collapsing back against the sparkling, white-tiled wall. My breaths wrenched shallow and fast from deep in my chest. I blinked, rapid-fire, wishing away the tears. Once they started, they might never stop.

I tried so hard to be strong. To be that woman who was tough and resilient and uncaring. A warrior who took no shit from anyone, who triumphed against adversity to fight another day.

All my bravado, all that hot air and unproven strength left me like air trickling from a leaky balloon. It bled from every muscle, every cell, every thought that said I wasn't the woman Richard scorned me to be.

I'd fought it—every day, in every part of my life, which threatened to cut me down and spit me out like worms from a rotting apple. But I was tired. So tired of living with this boulder strapped around my heart.

Sex made me forget. The bad sex, the battery-powered sex. Who the hell knew good sex would make me remember? Not only remember, but question and doubt every validation I reiterated, every day, every doubtful moment, before the negativity could settle in and fester.

I'd thought good sex was the answer. The way to make all the uncertainty drop away until I could believe in myself, in the idea that I deserved good as much as the next person.

I'd thought there was a way out of the spiral that made the men in my life want to hurt me, to make me suffer for whatever wrongdoing I'd imparted on their life.

I thought one day I'd be free from the past.

I was wrong.

6

GIDEON

The upside to working in your own private building is the peace and privacy. The downside to working on your own is . . . the peace and privacy. Silence yawned with the roar of an injured bear.

Thoughts of Tiff filled my head. Hot, cock-teasing thoughts, along with the memory of how good she felt until she wrenched herself away.

That was three sleepless nights ago.

The large clock on the lab wall said it was after nine pm. Brenda was long gone and hopefully the labs in the main building, particularly the specimen room, were unmanned.

I needed to oust thoughts of a certain blonde from my mind and remember why I'd been sent to Hagen Pharmaceuticals in the first place.

I left the lab's light on and the half-finished results of a test I'd started three days earlier. If I was found where I shouldn't be, the partially finished notes would provide my semi-believable excuse.

I'd already discovered who was working on the antidote.

Mannie. A large, lurid specimen who needed a good lesson in hygiene, mainly of the podiatry variety. Although the man may exhibit questionable personal care, his office and lab were meticulous. I'd searched both once already, and come up empty.

So, I'd befriended the man. Not hard. He wasn't inundated with company. A few strategically worded questions, and I discovered why my earlier searches had been fruitless. The serum antidote was stored in a second, higher security cold room.

I just needed to get in, get a sample and get out unnoticed.

Piece of cake.

The corridor glowed blue and I followed the security lights—and of course, the blue tiles—to the CDC lab. A vacant, void-like quality hung in the air. A quality that said I was alone.

Speed and stealth were what we did best, among other less savory pursuits. I reached the lab in barely two minutes and located the cold room soon after. It was then that I discovered yet another problem. I needed a code for the door, one that didn't match the one I used for the central cold storage.

Breaking in the door, much as I could with little effort, wasn't an option. No one could know the serum had been taken. Not if the mission was to succeed. Not if my race was to survive the genocide Hagen Pharmaceuticals had wittingly —or unwittingly—planned.

I had to find another way.

My senses pricked and I whirled around. A familiar, slim figure with rambling blonde curls was sneaking back down the corridor, no doubt in the hopes of avoiding me.

Not happening.

"Tiff."

She froze. Her shoulders lifted then dropped in an overstated "I'd rather scoop out my eyeballs than see you again" way.

Slowly, she turned. "I didn't realize anyone else stayed this late."

Dark circles rimmed eyes that had lost the sparkle and fire I'd glimpsed, was it only days earlier?

I moved closer, for no other reason than I'd missed the scent of her, the connection I felt with every cell in my centuries old body. "I wanted to set up some samples for a new test." Insight warred with conscience and I tamped the latter down. "Actually, maybe you can help."

She stumbled backwards, headlight-wide eyes once again avoiding my gaze. "I'm busy."

"Right now? I just need a couple of samples from the cold room, but my passcode won't work."

Her ramrod shoulders dropped. Marginally. "This room is restricted access, so only a few of us have the code." She skirted past me before moving toward the door.

I averted my eyes even as my ears pricked. She swiped her keycard and typed in her code. I took note, ignoring the growing unease prickling my gut. Our survival trumped everything, including any allegiance I felt for my soon-to-be-mate.

"What do you need?"

"*Strep pneumoniae.*"

She reclosed the door and stepped away. "You won't find that here. Streps are in the main storage."

"Damn, I must have missed it. I'll go back for another look."

Again that relief. That relaxing of muscles and soft, almost imperceptible sigh. "I'll leave you to it, then."

She'd done that for the past three days, since our near-thing in the sterility room, and it was driving me crazy. "Have dinner with me."

She stopped, but didn't turn. "No."

"Lunch?"

"No."

"Coffee, then."

"No. I told you." She turned and waved her hand between us. "I don't do this."

"By 'this' you mean me?"

Her eyes dropped, but not before I picked their haunted depths. "Yes."

"Why, Tiff?"

"It doesn't matter."

"It matters to me."

"It shouldn't. We barely know each other."

"I know enough." Doubt pierced her expression, quickly followed by denial.

She wouldn't discount the connection between us. Not when I sensed she felt it. Not when my whole mortality depended on it. "You can't judge what and how something affects me any more than I can for you." I stepped closer, inhaling air filled with her scent, then closer still, into her space, until my body responded to her heat, to the other half of what would make me whole. "I feel something when I'm with you, something I'd all but given up on feeling. If you don't feel it too, tell me and I'll let you be. But if you do feel it, all I ask is that you give this," I mimicked her wave between us, "give us a go."

Her gaze widened again, her body swaying in tune with

33

her indecision. And for a second, for one heady moment, I thought I'd dented her resolve. Then her expression slammed like a door in my face. "It's still no."

She turned, stalking with large, hurried steps towards her office at the far end of the corridor. "Don't forget to check the main doors lock behind you on the way out."

Then she was gone. Fleeing us. *Me*.

Again.

I didn't follow. What was the point? Something was holding her back and she wasn't ready to take a chance on us.

I'd soon change that. I had to. Only true sacrifice made in the name of true love could undo the curse. And I refused to remain cursed for another three centuries.

But before I could even contemplate *úspory*, our coupling, I had other, more pressing tasks to attend to. The task of fulfilling my destiny, and hers, would have to wait. And there was the little matter of how I had used her to gain the code to the cold store and the serum I needed. The knowledge slumped heavy in my chest, along with the knowledge that if she didn't come to me willingly, soulmate or not, my transformation wouldn't happen.

I needed time to convince her. And once upon a century, time was all I had. But since the discovery of the new, lethal Influenza A virus, and the world's subsequent scramble to prevent its spreading, the clock hands moved double time, and the longer I waited, the more likely our race would slip into extinction.

7

TIFFANY

I was fighting a losing battle. I could feel it. The
impulse. The temptation. The desire to throw all
sense to the wind and say yes.

It was just dinner.

Just lunch.

Just coffee.

Just that.

Harmless.

It didn't need to become more.

My shaking knuckles kneaded the pressure points either
side of my skull in an attempt to stem a pounding that
rivalled an elephant stampede. Avoiding Gideon was taking
its toll. Physically. Emotionally. Stretching me like a rubber
band, to the point of snapping.

I was better than that. Stronger. I didn't need to give in to
these urges and throw away three years of caution.

Yeah, right.

I'd be fooling myself if I believed any of it for a second.

Gideon made me feel something I couldn't define. Something foreign. Something real. Was it hope?

I had no idea. What I did know, was how dangerous he was to my equilibrium. To my sanity.

Just fuck him and when he disappoints like every other Tom, Dick or asshole, you'll exorcise him from your mind and move on.

It was food for thought.

Food for another day. Right now I needed out of the building. I had to head for home, away from temptation. My headache wouldn't budge, but a date with a long, cool cider and a good book would cure that.

I grabbed my helmet and headed for the bicycle shed, inhaling a deep breath of fresh air and fresh perspective. The air was damp, cold. Cobweb clearing. The bike ride home always soothed, refreshing my mind and invigorating my soul. And hopefully somewhere on the way, I'd pedal Gideon right out of my brain.

S o much for soothing. A flat frigging tire didn't even come close.

Half a mile into my two mile ride home, I'd felt the jolt of every stone, every crack on the road. I'd stopped, confirmed the worst, and began the long trek back to the lab.

A hot bath, a good book and an even better bottle of berry cider had dropped from "certainty" through to "impossible" and straight to "not happening anytime soon."

Of all the things I'd left behind when I left home, the taste for cider was one habit I couldn't kick.

I trudged, each step feeding my temper, driving my

mercury up and off the charts. Gideon fucking Fang. Somehow this was his fault. I'd ridden like a banshee, my only thoughts focused on increasing the distance between us.

I must have ridden over some nail, some glass, something that would have been noticeable if I hadn't still been steaming after our encounter.

Head down, temper seething, I mentally measured my distance from the lab. Ten minutes, max, till I arrived. I'd dump my bike, Uber it home and worry about fixing the tire tomorrow.

A sharp horn shafted through my thoughts. My head jerked up.

Damn.

The man I'd been trying—quite ineffectively—to escape. All leather and chrome and sexy and panty melting.

Fuck.

I was struggling to see a way out of this that didn't include getting into his pants—and out of mine. He cut the engine, lifted a denim-clad leg off the bike and joined me.

He spared me a glance. "Flat tires are the devil."

Takes one to know one.

I didn't comment. Maybe if I outright ignored him, he'd get the hint, wrap his Iron Man thighs back round his Harley and ride off, anywhere but in my vicinity.

"I think I saw a patch kit back at the lab if you need one."

Guilt whirled hand-in-hand with resentment. He was just being nice, and I was being a bitch. But I didn't want him to be nice. The nicer he was, the guiltier I felt for ignoring him. And that was all on him.

I hadn't asked him to stop.

Bitch.

My inner manners-meter chanted the word in my ears. *Bitch, bitch, bitch.*

"I'm a whiz at fixing tires." He shot me a grin. A cheeky, lava-warm grin. One that curved his lips and made me question what wonders they could wield on the buzzing flesh between my thighs.

Fuck me.

Yep, that was the only answer. Fuck him until I'd been there, done that, and could move on without wondering what he'd be like. I'd know, and reality wouldn't be half as good as the images whirling through my head. It never was.

Hagen Pharmaceuticals loomed up before us and I headed towards the bike shed. My body buzzed, hyperaware of his massive frame walking beside me.

I locked my bike and made for my office, his large, silent presence unnerving. I averted my gaze to the double sliding door entrance. Hopefully he'd get the hint and walk away.

The Harley's kickstand scraped the ground and his boots crunched over the pathway until he was within touching distance. My keycard was already in my hand, raised toward the sensor.

His burly, broad shoulders dropped. He sighed. "When are you going to stop ignoring the elephant in the room, Tiff?"

That made me stop. No ignoring him now. My hand dropped from the door and I spun around. "You want elephant? How about this?" I inhaled, deep, until my lungs threatened to burst. Then I blurted out the words before sense could pull them back. "One night, one fuck. No repeats, no mentioning it, *ever*. Agree and it happens right here, right now. No rainchecks. No second chances. You only get one, and this is it."

An entire movie of emotions trailed across his face, half of which I couldn't decipher. It didn't matter. This tryst, this little moment of madness, would be a one-off. I didn't need to know what he thought or felt. I just needed his agreement and his cock.

We'd fuck, move on, and I'd live with the disappointment that even god-like men like Gideon couldn't satisfy the need in me.

At least then I'd be able to return to Sammy and the roll of pleasure he'd delivered, unfailingly, till Gideon.

8

GIDEON

"Fuck me, Gideon."

The words jarred. Coarse and at odds with what I wanted.

Tiff and I weren't about fucking. We weren't just about the most elemental need of man and woman. What sparked between us was so much more.

An ancient legend, which had yet to reveal its truth to me. The love in Tiff's soul would call mine back. The act of giving, of sharing her body with mine, would make me whole again, free of the shackles binding me to an empty life and a future filled with blood-lust and madness. A future that awaited all vampires, care of one rogue gene, a cursed beginning, and a soulless existence. *The Change. Zmena.*

I wanted it all. To be saved, to be loved, to be real again.

What Tiff offered would be torture. A glimpse at what life could be, minus the rope to pull me from the spiral of my unchecked destiny.

Coupling without love wouldn't give me what I needed, yet I still felt her pull. The need to join and feel how good it was to be with the one Fate had chosen for me. One chance? If this was it, then I'd take it. The memory would last until the madness stole it and then it would be too late.

She was the only one to save me, yet maybe, somehow, I could save her right back. Hurt haunted her eyes, a deep distrust born from betrayal. Perhaps loving her would spark the feelings we needed to make our love work, till death do we part.

Who knew the immortal would crave death? Only, it wasn't death I craved. It was life before death. A meaning and fulfilment my existence lacked without my soul.

"Fuck me, Gideon."

Liquid ocean-blue eyes pleaded. She rested her palm on my chest and I wondered if she'd notice the missing beat of my heart. A heart only she could make beat again.

I took her keycard, opened the door and pulled her inside. There were too many cameras in the hallway, so I let her lead me to her office. The door snapped shut, and before she could change her mind, I plastered my body to hers and claimed her lips.

They opened readily and I drank, exploring her mouth just as I intended to explore every inch of her delectable body.

Sweet. Satisfying. Like that first, succulent sip of water after days of withering thirst.

Her hands squeezed my ass. My cock throbbed, ravenous.

My hands dropped to her hips and I lifted her, groaning as she wrapped me between her delectable legs, pushing her sweet pussy hard against my aching erection.

Lust and need coursed through my body. My cock wanted inside, but my mind wanted more.

I strode to her desk, swept her folders and papers aside and dropped her down. She lifted her arms and I made easy work of her tee. Next, her slacks, and barely-there lace that made my mouth water.

I pushed her knees apart, nostrils flaring with her scent, musk and butter and sugar-sweet arousal. Plump, pink flesh glistened wet with her need, inviting me in.

I fought the descent of my fangs. This wasn't a coupling. We were two humans stoking the fire that burned between us. I could be one of those humans for just one afternoon.

I ducked my head, hungry to taste her and pleasure her until she screamed my name and begged me to take her.

Her knees snapped shut and she grabbed a fistful of hair. "No tasting below the waist."

Lagoon-blue eyes flashed stormy and almost gray. She licked her lips and pulled my head up, proving there were more than enough offerings above the waist to occupy me.

Full, weighty breasts with nipples the shade of ripe, juicy plums begged for attention.

I ducked and tasted. Her body arched, pushing the ripe bud hard against my tongue. I cupped her breast and squeezed, stroking the tip with my tongue, sucking hard and deep, eliciting cries that darted with lightning-like precision straight for my throbbing cock.

Her hands fumbled with my jacket. I pulled back, dropped a condom onto the desk beside her, making light work of my clothes, all the while burning beneath her unabashed scrutiny. Her gaze followed the shedding of my clothes, from my chest, over my abs, down further still. It latched onto my erection and my cock pulsed as if her hands had wrapped round its girth and squeezed.

Then she sat up and did just that.

Fuck. Me.

"I fully intend to." Wet lips wrapped around the words, her eyes a wicked promise of delights to come.

I must have squeezed out the plea as her hand slipped down and squeezed my balls. Need surged inside, my balls so fucking tight, they'd well surpassed blue. I jerked free of her palm and slid on the condom. Her legs were already open and I pulled her delicious ass forwards, splaying her legs wider still, before sinking into her sweet, supple heat.

Fuck.

I closed my eyes and pushed back every one of my vampiristic inclinations, allowing whatever was left of the man I once was to take over. The feeling went beyond magical. Beyond anything dreams or legends had promised.

I was home.

9

TIFFANY

*W*ith one, swift motion, Gideon thrust into me. Solid, male muscle stretched me and filled me, his wondrous girth stroking my clit with every delicious slide in and out.

I gasped, wrapped my legs around his taut, beautiful body and tilted my hips, wanting more of him. All of him.

His eyes glowed green with flecks of shimmering gold. That hypnotic gaze bored into my soul, as his hard, thick cock pounded into my body. His fingers joined his cock, brushing that tight knot of nerves at my entrance and I almost leapt from my skin. Those sure, magical fingers found my G-spot and strummed my body into song. If I'd had spots A to F, damn straight, he'd have strummed music into them too.

I skimmed my hands up my body, palming my breasts, squeezing my nipples. They were so tight, so hard, intense pleasure bordering on pain.

His hands joined mine and my body spiraled. I'd never felt so hot, so horny, so much fucking sensation from one man. I wanted release, I didn't. I wanted to orgasm. I never wanted the sensation to end. It was a high bought from the purest of cravings.

He flicked a nipple and I squealed.

"Say my name."

It was an order, one barked through lips drawn tight with anticipation.

He flicked again, then squeezed, twisting the bud until I thought I might die from the pleasure. He thrust again, his thumb circling my clit, making me crazy. I closed my eyes and dropped my head back, slave to the sensation. To the hedonistic rapture Gideon milked from my body.

"Look at me and say my name, Tiff."

Something in that commanding, no-nonsense voice dragged my eyes open and tugged his name from my lips.

"*Gideon.*"

He tweaked and plucked my clit in time with each and every thrust. Fissures of sensation sparked through my body, exploding in orgasmic release that had me crying his name once again.

He growled, his cock pulsing as he unleashed into me. His power, his possession, frightening and fulfilling, all in one.

I clutched his taut, toned buttocks, stilling him, holding him deep as my body milked every last drop from his magnificent, pleasure-ridden cock.

A sigh escaped, rising out from every satiated cell. "Fuck me."

He grinned, that cocky, alpha male "I've got you right where I want you" grin, steeped in satisfaction and pure, male supremacy. "I believe I just did."

*E*very ounce of energy had zapped from my body. I was liquid. Lava. A languorous puddle of hedonistic gratification splayed across a desk I'd never be able to work on again.

Gideon fucking Fang.

Why him?

That supercilious smile made me want to slap him, then fuck him all over again. All fifty shades of fuckability.

Not happening. Not when this was a one-time thing. My words, my stipulations. And I had every intention of keeping them.

He withdrew that beautiful organ from my body and my pussy howled. His palm felt cool against my skin as it slid down towards the still thrumming flesh between my thighs.

"So fucking wet."

I was. Unheard of. Even Sammy didn't elicit half the response Gideon had.

Was still drawing from my spent body. One finger rubbed my G-spot, the other rubbed my super-sensitive clit. I was climbing again, and I hadn't even come down from before.

His gaze still glistened gold, his mouth clamped firmly closed, as if biting back his own arousal.

He dipped his head, mouth tugging and twirling my nipple, fingers pumping me until I screamed. Alpha or not, the man was anything but selfish. That encore was all about me.

And from his expression, the way his gaze fixated on my flesh still pulsing hungrily around his fingers, he wanted to give me more.

Fuck, yes.

I wanted his mouth there, his tongue fucking me until I forgot my name and every goddam reason why *this* should never have happened in the first place. And if sauce was involved—caramel or chocolate, I wasn't fussy—or even that dripping, thick honey, I wouldn't complain.

And there lay the basis why there would never—could never—be a repeat performance. Any more than a one or two night stand, and whatever was in me that made men hate—that made them lash out and hurt—would raise its ugly head and cause its evil havoc. I was helpless to stop it, so better I didn't let its spiral begin.

Now was the moment to scrape myself up, dust myself off, thank him for the orgasm of my life, then move on. If only my legs weren't sticks of jelly and my mind wasn't so scrambled it was even now trying to devise a way to make this less of a finale and more of an *hors d'Oeuvre*.

Stupid bitch.

Richards words, but at this precise moment, I believed them.

The moment was beyond morning after awkward.

I scooched back, away from those magic fingers, and pushed up, closing my legs to that orgasm-triggering gaze.

He turned away, his shoulders stiffening, his ragged breathing slowing. When he turned back again, his eyes were more green than gold, and his expression had shuttered.

Clothes littered the floor, mine intermingled with his. I scrambled down and grabbed my shirt, tossing him his briefs. His still exposed, still semi-aroused cock would be my undoing. He needed to cover up and give me breathing space to think and reason, and leave before I did something stupid, like beg for an encore.

Gideon fucking Fang.

The bastard made me want things I hadn't believed possible since I was a teen.

Stupid bitch.

Would I never learn?

I had to go.

"So, how are we going to do this?" That deep, sex-curling voice wound through my thoughts and tugged.

My shirt was on, my g-string tight and rubbing against flesh still singing from his rip-roaring assault. I dragged up my pants and focused on the mess of papers and pens on the floor. "Do what?"

"Work together when we know how good we can be."

"Sex is just sex, Gideon." I spared his now jeans-clad body a glance. "Don't confuse what we just did for more."

My inner goddess winced, her post-orgasmic glow at odds with my words.

His lips twisted in what I could only label as distaste. Something deeper, darker, flickered in his eyes. I felt his scrutiny, as if his very being were burrowing deep into my brain.

Silence clamored against my eardrums. The world receded, leaving nothing but me and the heat smoldering between us.

My heart stuttered.

I swallowed, drawn to him by some invisible thread. A pull that made me take one crawling step towards him.

He shook his head and dragged his gaze from mine, slipping into his jacket, scrunching his sexy black t-shirt in his big, magical hand. "If you can't tell the difference between sex and more, then you're not the woman I thought you were."

With that—and my heart ricocheting rebelliously in my chest—he turned and silently slipped through the door.

THE DARK SIDE

With jigan—and any other dragon magnanimously in the air—he roamed and silently slipped through the forest

10

GIDEON

*T*here were so many elements of wrong in what I was about to do.

My hand slipped into my pocket, and wrapped around Tiff's keycard—the solution to my restricted area access problem. I could now move freely within all areas of Hagen Pharmaceuticals' main building, restricted or otherwise. Then, of course, she'd handed me access to the restricted cold room when she'd entered the code within hearing range.

And if my gut twisted around the morals of my actions, I just had to consider the consequences of *not* acting, of Mannie's serum entering production, and the gradual genocide of my kind.

Vampires.

From the beginning of time, we'd fallen victim to a string of nefarious legends. Labeled murderers. Rogues of the night. Slaves to a bloodlust and enemy to all mankind.

In truth, we're a race trapped in a living hell by an ancient curse. Yes, we feast on blood's iron-richness to survive. And, yes, we can kill and turn others through *zahŕňa*. Most sane, pre-changed vamps recoil at the thought, which is why we're primarily a dying race—an ironic contradiction for a clan seemingly afflicted with immortality.

But that immortality comes at a price.

For those of us fortunate enough to find our soulmate and undergo *úspory*, we reclaim our souls and live relatively normal, mortal lives. For those not so lucky, two alternatives exist—termination of our undead life via a mercy killing, or finally surrendering to *zmena*—an eternity wandering the earth beneath a veil of uncontrollable madness and blood-lust.

The newly discovered flu super virus presented a graver third alternative. With its rapid airborne spreadability worldwide, the World Health Organization had jumped in, feet first, proposing a comprehensive, quick-fix solution—release the new antidote into the air and facilitate blanket immunization.

The Greens and environmentalists loudly protested, but global panic had won out.

In less than two weeks, production would begin, ready for a coordinated worldwide release. All in order to prevent the predicted, worldwide pandemic.

It all seemed so tidy and neat—beat an airborne virus with another airborne virus. Save the world.

But for one, unforeseeable hitch—the antidote's active protein irreversibly inactivates a vamp's "soul" gene. And the moment it does, we undergo *zmena*. Our psychosis is swift and severe, sparking a blood frenzy to rival any zombie apocalypse. The result of which would eventually lead to the extinction of both races.

For the sake of my species, and for the sake of the humans with whom we coexist, something had to be done.

Hence, my duplicity towards Tiff was justified.

The reasoning still didn't quash the unease in my gut.

I flashed the keycard at the sensor and pushed through the glass door. Only two hours since we'd entered these doors together, then I'd entered Tiff and totally lost myself in the process. We may not have performed *párovan*—the pairing ritual that would see me saved—but something in me felt irrevocably linked to her.

My life—regardless of the madness that awaited if we didn't pair—would never be the same again.

I stopped outside the cold room. Only the whirr of the motor and an intermittent buzz of one of the hallway lights cut through the calm.

I swiped the keycard, entered the code and pulled open the door. It didn't take long to find the master serum. Normally I'd have no need for gloves or a mask— immortality had its advantages. But this time I donned both. Using a syringe, I transferred a sample into a vial from my pocket, then replaced the master just as I'd found it. Within minutes I was exiting the building and heading for my bike. I needed to get the sample to our lab so the techies could get started on creating an alternative.

Ours wasn't the only mission. Each and every known lab worldwide had been infiltrated. Every known antidote would be tested, and once relevant alternatives were derived, the master antidotes would be replaced and the formula altered. If all went to plan, no one would be the wiser. Spread of the virus would be curtailed, and vamps could continue to roam the earth, undisturbed. Unproven to man outside of folklore and legends.

Meantime, I was to wait for instructions, ingratiating

myself deeper into Mannie's life, allowing me access to his formula if and when it was needed.

Thankfully, not a full-time pursuit.

That gave me time to strategize how to convince Tiff we were more than a one-night fuck.

11

TIFFANY

*B*efore meeting "he who shall not be named," there was only one thing I hated more than arriving late for work—arriving late, only to discover I'd misplaced my keycard.

Now, since that fateful meeting, only one hate trumped even that. It was suspecting that said keycard had fallen somewhere on my office floor while Gideon and I had done what we shouldn't, what even now refused to stop replaying over and over in my mind.

A recalcitrant throb started up between my thighs. A throb that said my body wanted more than just the memory.

Yeah. That hate trumped any I could come up with.

Or so I thought, till I checked on my bike and found it where I'd left it. Punctureless.

Gideon fucking Fang.

Bad enough I'd fucked the guy, I didn't want to like him as well.

I was off to a rip-roaring start to the day. I'd slept

through my alarm, no doubt because I hadn't sunk into sleep until just before dawn. *Thank you, Gideon.* My Uber had taken a record fifteen minutes to arrive, leaving me with no time to pick up a coffee on the way. Then I'd madly hunted through my purse and pockets only to discover a pack of sugar-coated gummy bears had spilled all through my bag, and no keycard.

After more than a few unsavory epithets, I'd called Mannie to let me in—given he always started as early, if not earlier, than me. I'd not appreciated his expression as we'd walked down the main corridor together. Another mark against Gideon.

My keycard was lying under my desk. Less than a foot from the spot where we'd fucked each other's brains out.

The coffee machine in the break room wasn't working and I couldn't fix my mind on work and off Gideon's cock pounding pleasure into my body.

Mark number three going on thirty.

I was absolutely and totally fucked. Thank fuck it was Friday—at least one good wave in a sea of bedlam. I slumped further into my ergonomic office chair and banged my head on my desk. Perhaps in the process, I'd knock some sense into my brain.

What the fuck was I supposed to do?

"Soy latte with one sugar, right?"

My gaze shot from the aroma-rich takeaway cup to the man offering it to me.

Need shivered through my blood.

Gideon fucking Fang.

I don't know what was worse. The fact he'd paid attention enough to know my beverage of choice, the fact he'd sensed my lack of caffeine and acted on it, or the fact he looked so fuckable—and damned well likeable—handing me a coffee in my moment of need.

I took the cup from his outstretched hand. It would have been churlish—and stupid, given my caffeine-starved body —not to.

"Thanks." The word rasped from my desert-dry mouth.

His grin sent me fifty shades of hot and horny. I clamped my thighs and lifted the cup to my lips.

"Is the coffee machine here always so unreliable?" He perched on my desk, sipping from his own cup, his thick, muscular thigh stretching the limits of tight, black denim. *Fuckola.* Denim over a hot bod was like hot fudge sauce over pretty much anything.

Irresistible.

Once again, Gideon made my mind wander to sauce. And how I wanted it slathered over my body so he could lap it up with his masterful tongue.

Need, hot and thick, swamped my veins. I knocked back a mouthful of coffee, scalding my tongue in the process. Just desserts for entertaining such flagrant, forbidden thoughts. He was off limits, as were any notions of revisiting last night's activities.

"Tiff?"

My gaze slid towards that rich-as-honey voice. "Ah, yeah." I cleared my throat. I'd been speaking since well before I could walk. Why was it so difficult now? "It has a knack for timing."

He nodded. Didn't comment on why I'd need coffee more this morning than any other. My Gideon like-o-meter edged upwards.

56

"What are you working on?"

That was easy. Unemotional. Non-personal. Safe. "Mannie asked me to glance over his draft notes on the Influenza A antidote. He has one more test before the final report is due to the HHS late next week and a fresh pair of eyes is always useful when editing." And he couldn't send it unchecked to the US Department of Health and Human Services. Hence, I'd been asked to step in and do what I do best. Make the senior, male members of our lab look good.

Bitter much? Yeah, well I had every reason.

Again Gideon nodded, acting as if every one of my words were the most interesting he'd heard all morning. My GLOM edged up a few more notches.

"Did you hear Mannie's taking up a senior scientist position in WHO after this project?"

"Yeah, I heard."

"Going to apply for his position?"

I'd considered it . . . until sense kicked in and I realized that Graeme would never place me in a position where his own would be threatened.

To an onlooker, it seemed like stupidity for me to stay at Hagen when I was thwarted every which way, every time I tried to move up. That's because they didn't see the good in my job. How our private lab offered something most government labs didn't—an environment beyond Richard's ever-reaching grasp.

That was the long answer, one which Gideon didn't need to know. Suffice to say, he could make do with the shorter, brush-off version. "I'll think about it."

"If you apply, I'd be happy to back your recommendation."

Whoa! My heart beat double-time and my GLOM pushed to the max. I had to cut this conversation off at the knees, before I dropped to mine and begged him to take me again.

"That won't get you back into my pants."

His expression cut my snide retort off at the calves. It was low, when all he'd done was offer me kindness. But I didn't want kindness, not from him. I didn't want anything that made him more likeable and more fuckable, and gave little or no arguments to stop me from doing both.

"Much as I'd love back into your pants, my offer had nothing to do with that. You're good at your job, much better than some, and I believe Graeme would be an idiot not to consider you for the position."

Fuck.

I was so, so gone.

"Thanks. That's really nice of you to say."

"I didn't say it because it was nice. I said it because it's true. I still question why my job wasn't handed to you."

I'd long since stopped questioning, after seeing how good he was at what he did. Still, it was nice of him to say. "Yeah, well, if I'd landed the position, we'd all have missed your scintillating company."

"Imagine that." He grinned, and without thinking, my lips curved in response. "I can't say I'm sorry. Meeting you has been a highlight." He raised his hand. "And before your panties get all knotted into thinking that comment is about last night, I just want to clarify that it is, but it's also about much more. This moment, right now, and every other time we've talked and I've felt at one with you."

The man knew how to melt every item of clothing—panties included—clear from my body. I wanted to believe him. Everything in me wanted to trust that I was more than the sum of Richard's bitter aspersions.

There was a word. *Trust.* I'd sworn it'd be a cold day in hell before I handed that sword over to a man again. Yet here I was, wondering if Gideon could be the one.

Was I stupid for thinking he wouldn't take my trust and ram it straight through my heart?

Richard's actions had made me bleed—in truth, I was bleeding still. Was I really ready to try again?

He knocked back the last of his coffee and lobbed the empty cup into the recycle box next to my trash. When he turned back and his green gaze met mine, flutters filtered out from my chest, burrowing deep down into my abdomen.

I swallowed.

Damn. Even a brow-quirk was sexy on Gideon. "That wasn't so bad, was it?"

I pulled my mind back from his sexy eyebrow to decipher his comment. "The coffee?"

"Coffee with me." His lips slid into a sexy, fuck-me-six-ways-through-Sunday smile. "Isn't the next step lunch? Or we could miss that one and go straight to dinner."

Temptation incarnate. He was like the devil, dangling all my hopes and dreams just out of reach. "It's only dinner, Tiff. I'm not asking for more."

Problem was, I wasn't adverse to him asking for more. I was just too damn scared to give it. And I hated it. Hated that Richard's claws were still firmly sunk into my soul.

Still, he was right. It was only dinner. And dinner didn't have to lead to more if I didn't want it to.

His gaze bored holes in my every resolve, his patience warming every part of me not already burning with anticipation. That sexy, pleasurable mouth curved into what I could only describe as a hopeful smile.

I blocked every warning that stated I was being a fool once again.

Only dinner, I could do.

"Sure. Why not?"

12

GIDEON

*T*t wasn't the most enthusiastic of responses, but it was a start.

We'd moved from a cold standoff, through coffee, to all the possibilities a shared dinner promised. And much as I'd be lying if I said I didn't want the evening to end balls-deep inside her sweet body, that wasn't the extent of my need where Tiff was concerned. I enjoyed our exchanges, enjoyed picking the moment in each one where she finally relaxed and let me in. I wanted inside of her head as much as I wanted inside of her body, to discover what made her delectable mind tick. I wanted her body and soul, both of which would only come with trust and an openness that until now had been lacking between us.

Tonight was my opportunity to change that.

We'd agreed to meet at Greco's, a new restaurant in the French Quarter, not far from Woldenberg Park. I'd insisted on picking her up, she'd insisted on meeting me there. I'd eventually conceded, and clocked it up to a win. I understood how important it was to retain a semblance of control. I felt the same when bloodlust hit. Losing control meant losing a sense of myself, and it cut too close to the core and a future I dreaded with every ounce of my being.

I turned back to the bar and ordered, the vodka and lime springing more from habit than need. My taste buds wouldn't appreciate the drink's flavor any more than they'd appreciate the food we were about to eat. For three hundred years, nothing but blood had seen them waken. But a lifetime of fitting in meant I ate and drank when social etiquette required it.

And for the purposes of now, drinking gave me something to do while I waited for Tiff to arrive.

A sudden awareness zapped up my spine. I turned and immediately found her. Even across the room I sensed her uncertainty—fight warring with flight as she reluctantly weaved around tables to join me at the bar.

A black, ankle-length skirt with an ass-high side-slit swished about her black boots, the sparkles on her black top glinting under the golden drop lights. Nothing particularly tight or revealing, but for the split that barely winked my way. I'd bet my Harley she'd chosen them deliberately, with lack of seduction in mind. She seemed unaware that covering up that beautiful body was just as alluring as revealing it. I'd sampled the delights beneath all that black, and nothing, no mourner's outfit, could detract from the memory.

"Hi." I moved a little to make space for her beside me.

She eyed the small gap, then determinedly remained where she was. "Hi." She breathed the word between pants, as if she'd run the distance from her tiny apartment, two blocks away. "Sorry I'm late."

I bit back a trail of cheesy replies from *you're worth the wait,* to *the best things in life are worth waiting for.* "I booked a table, but would you like a drink here first?" Again that uncertainty. I could read each thought as it tumbled through her mind and across her overly expressive face. Primarily, they all boiled down to one question—did she want to extend the evening by sharing a drink now?

She barely paused with her answer. "Let's sit."

If I were one to read between the lines, I'd be sure to read "the sooner we're done, the better." Just as well that wasn't my thing.

I dropped my hand to her waist, leading her to the left and our semi-private, corner table.

Tiff chose the seat with her back to the wall, leaving me with my back to the restaurant. I shuffled my chair to the left, allowing my peripheral vision to take in the other tables around us. What it also did was bring me close enough to breath in her heady scent—vanilla and spice and all things sexy.

In the low lighting, her eyes glowed deep, dark cobalt and her cheeks were dusty pink. She licked her lips and I wanted to do the same. I swallowed. "You look beautiful."

Her gaze narrowed. "Thanks."

I bit back a sigh. How to disprove her so obvious skepticism? I had two options—let her continue to doubt everything I said, or cut her disbelief off at the knees before it had a chance to grow. No choice, really.

"Before the evening goes any further, let's get one thing straight." I covered the hand scrunching her napkin on the table. She snatched it free. I swallowed another sigh, fighting to keep the frustration from my voice. "Saying you're beautiful wasn't a line or an attempt to lead you on. I genuinely find you shit-hot sexy and totally irresistible." I shot her a grin. "And in the essence of all-out honesty, I also find you interesting. So, much as I'd love another rendition of last night's activities, I also want to get to know you. That means genuine, straight-down-the-line conversation, no bullshit." I tried to read between her crinkled brows and her tightly clamped lips, her sharply squared shoulders and stiffly raised chin, and got nothing. "So, Tiff. What do you say?"

I sipped my drink, biting my tongue, leaving her space and time and the power to choose whichever direction the evening would take.

After an age, her shoulders dropped and she pinned her gaze to mine. "No bullshit and *no* sex. Just conversation."

"That's all I ask."

"That's all you're getting."

I nodded. If she wanted a rise, she wouldn't get one. Not above the waist, that is.

Silence rose up and yawned between us, despite the animated chatter from nearby tables and the louder than necessary tones of AC/DC riding the highway to hell.

There was so much we had to learn about each other, so much *she* had to learn. We were fated to be together, till death do we part, and she had to come willingly. That meant trust, on both sides.

Something that wouldn't happen if we didn't get past the burgeoning black hole that had completely killed conversation.

I needed to act before the evening moved from awkward to irreparable.

"Smooth or crunchy?"

Her head snapped back. The wary, deer caught in headlights look vanished, surprise taking its place. And a

64

question, no doubt along the lines of whether I'd lost every one of my marbles.

Our relationship wasn't destined for ordinary. Why should our conversation be any different?

"W—what?"

"Smooth or crunchy, as in peanut butter. Which are you?"

"Why?" Still no trust, and the conversation was on *spreads*.

We'd get past this if it killed me. I ignored the reality of the throwaway and focused on the depths of her blue-green gaze. "Because it's more interesting than 'what's your favorite color?' and less risky than 'top or bottom? What's your favorite position?'"

13

TIFFANY

*J*ust when I thought I had Gideon all figured out, he threw me a curveball.

Peanut butter.

The question almost made me smile, as did his reasons for it. Bite or not to bite? The answer was simple. I didn't want this uncomfortableness between us any more than I wanted him out of my pants. Not really.

At least the discomfort I could do something about.

I inhaled and met his gaze with one just as sharp. "Neither. I'm a Nutella kinda girl."

He nodded. "Ahh, choc-nut. Interesting."

"Is it?"

"Everything about you is interesting."

Yeah, right.

The tone behind the words seemed sincere, perhaps he even believed them, but what compliment ever came without strings?

"Cilantro, yes or no?"

The question broke my thoughts and I left them.

Whatever his motivation, it wasn't my concern as long as it didn't suck me in. "Yes, of course. Thai food isn't the same without it." I thought quickly. "White or black pepper?"

"Black. I like the complexity." He raised his brows. "You?"

"White. I guess I'm just a simple gal at heart."

He didn't comment. And for that I was relieved, much as it would have given me more reason to doubt him. I needed it, but wasn't sure I wanted it.

"I'd ask snow or sunshine, but I already know you prefer snow." He considered. "Beach or pool?"

"Pool. Sand's too messy."

"Agreed."

I couldn't resist. "Blondes or brunettes?"

"Either. Hair color is incidental, personality is what cuts it for me."

I couldn't help the jump of my brows. *Really?*

"Hey, I promised no bullshit and I meant it." He grinned. "I could have taken the cheesy route and said blondes, especially the one opposite me, but I didn't. Give credit where credit's due." The sexy curve of his lips almost undid me more than his words.

Fuck.

An unfortunate choice of words when Gideon was near.

He moved forwards and drummed the table with his fingers. "Waffles or pancakes?"

"No competition. Pancakes."

He nodded before scanning the restaurant floor. "Our wait staff seem awfully absent." He cocked his head. "How hungry are you?"

An unfortunate question. But he wasn't talking anything but food. The subtext was all me. "Fair but not ravenous."

"Good." He took my hand, and this time I didn't snatch it back. His skin was cool, yet he still managed to warm my blood. "Trust me?"

It was a long shot, and I could only jump so far. I spared him a faint smile. "Where dinner's concerned, I'll take a leap."

"Good." Although his expression didn't match the word. Still, this was a night for no bullshit, and that saloon door swung both ways.

"Let's go." He pulled me up, and I let him, grabbing my bag as he swept me out of the restaurant and onto the street. With no time to catch my breath, he kept jogging, I kept following, glad I wore boots instead of skimpy heels and an even skimpier skirt.

"Where are we going?"

"Have faith. I won't lead you astray."

I doubt that.

We barely paused for traffic, crossing the street, turning the corner, leaving the brilliance and buzz of the restaurant behind. The sidewalk shimmered golden under the glow of street lamps, undertones of fall nipping the air with frost.

My breath escaped in pants, short and fast and oxygen-starved, creating misty white clouds that dissipated moments after they formed. Gideon seemed barely affected. The man had stamina plus—another thought that sent my imagination spiraling.

He pulled me into a dimly lit alley and I pulled back, heart jackhammering against my ribs. "I don't do alleys."

He shot me a look as if I was half-baked. I returned the look. I also wasn't born yesterday. He'd promised no sex, but he hadn't said nix on the seduction.

"Roll with this. You won't regret it." When I still hesitated, he added, "No bullshit, I promise."

I must be a stark-raving idiot, or at the very least, TSTL. But too stupid to live or not, I let him lead me into the dark. Funny thing was, a couple of seconds in, we reached a brightly-lit all-night café. I'd walked past this alley on countless occasions and never knew what existed beyond its entrance.

He paused at the door. "They make the best pancakes, ever."

"Pancakes for dinner?"

"Why not? Live a little dangerously, Tiff."

Problem was, I'd been there, done that and the battered, blood-soaked tee was an everlasting reminder of my mistake.

I shook off all thoughts of Richard. That bastard would not ruin tonight.

While every voice in my head screamed out warnings, I focused on Gideon's golden gaze and dragged in a much needed dose of oxygen.

It's just pancakes, for fuck's sake. "Sure. Why not?"

We pushed into the café and despite the fact that it was buzzing and fuller than I'd have expected due to its out-of-the-way location, we found a booth towards the back. I scooched in and he followed, only stopping when his thigh was firmly plastered against mine. Good lord, it felt good. Just a touch, and blood sizzled through my veins.

He seemed not to notice, handing me a menu from the center of the table, then leaning over to examine it rather than getting his own.

God, he smelled good. Like fresh, rambling cornfields, crisp pine needles and a dash of lime or lemon, I couldn't tell which.

"It doesn't matter which pancake you choose, they're all good." He ran a trim, tanned finger down the menu then stopped halfway down. "I'm thinking *Date Night*."

"They're movie titles!"

"Just a bit of fun. Jet, the owner, is a movie buff. So everything on the menu has a movie slant."

"*Mad Max* mega burger?"

"To die for, but we're here for pancakes." His glance slid from the menu to me. "Unless you fancy a burger? I can highly recommend the Dirty Harry double beef. Or even the Charlton Heston chicken burger if you're poultry inclined."

"It's ridiculous."

"Perhaps. But it's also a bit of fun." He returned his gaze to the menu. "*It Happened One Night* is looking pretty good right now." He waggled his brows, and I couldn't help but grin back. "Or maybe you prefer *Some Like it Hot*?"

"I'm leaning towards *The Good, The Bad and the Ugly*."

His gaze raked mine. "*Picture Perfect*."

"*Stepford Wives*."

"*Taming of the Shrew*."

"*Single White Female*."

"*Redemption*."

"*Psycho*."

"I'm sensing a theme here. Should I be worried?"

It was my turn to waggle my brows. "Very."

He chuckled, deep and decadent. The timbre burrowed deep into my gut and sank right down to the tips of my curling toes. If ever there was a fuck-me sound that saw my pussy wet and swooning, that was it.

His body was so close, we were almost touching. And that *almost* was killing me.

He pushed the menu my way. "What say we get a selection? Your choice."

"Any preferences?"

"Nope." He leaned back, crossing his arms, watching me beneath hooded lids. "I trust you."

I blinked, staring down at the blurring black print, hoping he didn't spot my weakness. It was such a silly, ridiculous thing. He trusted me to order. It shouldn't have meant something, not even remotely, yet my tummy flipped and fluttered as if he'd given it wings.

And I was too damn taken in to let it bother me.

Gideon fucking Fang.

The man was melting my resolve the way chili-chocolate sauce would melt all over *Como Agua Para Chocolate's* raspberry and mango compote.

My body heated, as if that very sauce were sinuating through my blood.

Gideon may have promised to behave, but right now, I wished he hadn't.

T wenty possible pancake creations and I had to choose. It was like dropping a kid into Walmart and telling her to pick only three toys.

I *ummed* and *ahhed*, and Gideon laughed and teased, but not once did he try and sway me.

I ignored the warmth fluttering through my chest, finally deciding on *The Dark Knight* chocolate berry wonder, the *Pulp Fiction* salted caramel popcorn and almond-vanilla bean ice cream, and the *Herbie Goes Bananas* banana rum and raisin pecan brittle. Three pancakes with two spoons. We topped it off with a double accompaniment of choc wild berry and caramel smoothies. A sugar-rush that would see me struggling to sleep for days.

I refused to care.

A couple nodded in greeting as they passed our table, hip-to-hip, arm-in-arm. Gideon grinned and nodded back.

Everyone seemed to know everyone, patrons and staff. Perhaps it was a result of the café being off the beaten track. Only those aware of its existence could find it. People stopped at our table, or waved from a distance. The waitress seemed more than familiar with Gideon, and as they chatted, jealousy hit me square in the chest. I hit it right back. I had no reason to feel that useless emotion, least of all for a man who was nothing more than a casual fuck.

The glib throwaway didn't sit easily on my conscience, but I knocked that feeling right back too. Emotions weren't a luxury I should—or would—allow myself.

"Do I detect a Kiwi accent?"

My hand froze, a forkful of chocolate and berries floating perilously in the air. "Maybe." I stuffed the fork in my mouth, the decadence tasting like dust. It had taken years to lose that last link to my childhood, and somehow he'd picked it up anyway. "How did you guess?"

"I have an ear for languages and sounds." He grinned. "So, why the move to New Orleans?"

I didn't go there. *Ever.* I was a NOLA girl now, through and through. He didn't need the ins and outs, the who, whys and wheres of my decision.

Diversion was my best option. "You speak more than one language?"

"Twenty-one. But that doesn't include dialects."

"Fuck me."

His brows arched, lips sliding into a salacious smile. "Is that an invitation?"

I ignored the rejoinder, just as much as I ignored the heat that followed it. "How the hell did you find the time to learn them all?"

"Once you know two or three, learning gets easier."

"Right." I groaned. "Feeling quite inadequate here, with my meager, one language ability. I don't know what I've been doing with my life."

He chuckled. "Science is a language."

"It's not the same. You're like a walking Google translator." I sipped my smoothie and contemplated the enigma opposite me. "I won't ask for a list, that'd be too depressing. What's the weirdest language you know?"

"Hah. That'd have to be Klingon."

I swallowed a snort, and ended up spluttering instead. "Is that even a real language?"

"It is for all the Klingons out there."

"Ha ha." Gideon's humor rubbed elbows with mine. He was spontaneous. Fun. Unpredictable in a way that shivered up my spine and weakened my knees. Good or bad, I was still undecided. That didn't stop me from playing while I made up my mind. "Say something."

He did that whole sexy brow-arching thing again, his gaze burrowing deep into mine. Then he cocked his head. *"Nuq wab chenmoH naHlet HeghDI' chuy chaH?"*

Whoa. I'd totally believed he was joking. "Sounds dirty. What does it mean?"

"What sound do nuts make when they sneeze?"

I snorted a laugh. I'd totally expected some cheesy line, and he'd surprised me. Again. "That sounded so much better in Klingon."

He grinned back. "Want the answer?"

"Enlighten me."

"Cash-ew."

I couldn't help but roll my eyes. "Lame."

"Would quoting Shakespeare have impressed you more?"

"Oh, don't worry, I'm impressed. Even quoting Baa Baa Black Sheep would have been effective."

He snagged a fork of banana and I did the same.

Funny, the conversation waned, but the silence was far from stilted. It sizzled. I wanted Gideon, in the most basic of ways. And this time I wasn't stupid enough to think one time would cut my cravings.

More than a single repeat performance was called for. And why not?

My heart stuttered at the thought, even while the heat in my veins sizzled.

I'd been rash in my "no sex, just talk" proviso for the evening. Sex was where I felt comfortable, where everything fit perfectly into place—pun one-hundred and ten percent intended.

Conversation and heart-to-hearts were the root of all troubles.

I was older, wiser. Some might say jaded, I'd say judicious. I was no longer the naïve, pliable fool I'd been in the past. I could spot the signs and cut our . . . whatever we were doing, short if so much as a hint of anger raised its ugly head.

I was bruised, not broken. Sex had been my sanity for the past three years. Why should I forgo the best experience of my life over a possibility? The change might never happen.

Richard's smirk, ugly and taunting, rose up before me.

Stupid bitch.

I pushed that face and the burgeoning doubts back down.

It wasn't the sex that was the problem. Never the sex. It was all the other stuff that landed me in trouble. Well, if Gideon didn't know me, then he couldn't hate me. And better still, he'd never need to hurt me.

14

GIDEON

I'd promised Tiff no sex, but goddam, she was testing that promise.

Her scent filled my nostrils, her every heartbeat pounded in my ears. I wanted to take her and taste her until she lost every bit of control and screamed my name. She topped a fork with chocolate dipped raspberries and whipped cream then slid it between her parted lips.

Fuck me.

I bit back a groan and stuffed a forkful of something—hell only knew what—into my mouth. Her thigh brushed mine and my cock jerked. Any minute now, I'd grab her and to hell with the consequences.

I swallowed and focused on the dregs of our three pancakes. She'd made it quite clear personal was off the table and I wasn't about to break my balls trying to change that. I'd try another tack. "What's your all-time favorite movie?"

She licked her lips then slowly curved them upwards. "Yours first."

I dragged my attention from those lips to her tropical lagoon gaze. My scrambled mind could barely focus beyond the tightness in my balls. I bit out my answer. "Easy. Anything with a Marvel in front of it."

"Figures."

"What? I'm that predictable?" Of course I was. I'd tossed her a cliché. Her response was reasonable. My less-than-enamored reaction for it wasn't.

She raised her brows. "What man doesn't long to be a hero, even if only in his mind?"

I barked out a laugh. "Harsh."

"Perhaps, but true."

A generalization. Again, perfectly reasonable. What one didn't know, one hypothesized. It was human nature, this need for super-human action and strength.

Vamps were of another cloth.

We didn't wear capes or fly about saving distressed heroines, but we could leap from tall buildings in a single bound. We could also terminate the life of a killer or rapist and sustain our hunger in the process. The blood may not be as sweet, but the guilt wasn't as sharp, either. Whether or not that made us a hero was up for debate.

Either way, we didn't fit the cliché of beasts of the night, transforming into bat form, feeding on innocents to slake our blood thirst. For the most part, we were a race surviving the only way we knew how, searching tirelessly for a way out of our living hell.

"Don't tell me that as a kid you never wanted to be Superman."

I wouldn't tell her. She wouldn't believe me.

It had been three hundred years since I'd been a kid, at a time when the likes of Voltaire, Benjamin Franklin and John

Quincey Adams were idols. Men didn't waltz around in capes unless they were mad or a Shakespearean actor.

Yeah, not an answer she'd understand.

"Not Superman. The Lone Ranger."

"Ahh, so you have a Harley in lieu of a horse?"

I couldn't help but grin. "I guess you could draw that analogy. What's your favorite, then?" I speared a chunk of pecan brittle-topped banana and waved the fork her way. "Don't tell me." I studied her face and got nothing. So I took a stab. "Pride and Prejudice."

Her lips twisted. "Not likely."

"Enlighten me."

"Frances Ha."

She said the name as if I'd no chance in hell of knowing it. She wasn't wrong.

"Never heard of it."

"It's not mainstream. There are no superpowers or superhuman battles."

"What's it about?"

She tilted her head, a little like a bird contemplating how to attack a worm. "One woman's journey to learn who she is before she can become who she should be."

"Deep."

"Authentic."

"So, not a romance."

The shake of her head was categorical. "Not even close."

"Don't most movies have at least a hint of romance?"

"Not the real ones."

There had to be a clue somewhere in that statement. Something to provide insight into the whole "fucking without friendship" thing she had going. "You think romance isn't real?"

78

"Oh, it's real all right. It's just less raindrops on roses and more sex with strings, stupidity and a dash of exploitation."

The words cut, regardless that the rationale didn't relate to me. "Wow. Where does love fit into all that?"

"It doesn't. It fits into my world about as much as unicorns and vampires."

She barely blinked as the statement left her lips. I wasn't sure what should have annoyed me more—her flippancy over my existence or her adamant disbelief in love. Both jeopardized my future. *Our shared future.*

Unless I could convince her she was wrong on both accounts.

Her thick lashes fluttered, her gaze fixed to mine as she slicked moisture across her lips. "What does fit into my world is very hot, very dirty, very immediate sex." She squeezed my thigh, her fingers digging into flesh just shy of my straining cock.

Was it a test? The few still operational brain cells couldn't fathom another reason for her behavior. And they didn't particularly care.

I wanted her fingers there, and higher, cupping and squeezing, her mouth sucking and fucking my aching dick until I exploded.

Thoughts that weren't helping me retain control.

I wanted this, but I wanted our shared future more. If I slipped up now, any chance of winning Tiff, of winning her trust, would be as short-lived as a virgin in a brothel.

I grabbed her hand and threaded her fingers through mine, dragging them away from my cock and insufferable temptation.

Luckily, or not so luckily, Jet chose that moment to leave

his double-grill for a snoop and a chat. "Gideon. How's it hanging, bro?"

Normally I'd stand and we'd man-hug, but certain bodily *impediments* made it impractical. Unless I wanted Jet to believe I suddenly preferred cocks over clits.

We fist bumped and he dropped onto the cushion beside me, eyeing Tiff with interest I wanted to punch square in the face. "Hey, I'm Jet."

She nodded, brandishing him with a smile that pricked at every nerve I owned. "Tiffany."

I elbowed his ribs, regaining his attention. "Pancakes were perfect, as usual."

He stroked his impeccably manicured moustache. "Of course."

The man was anything but humble. With good reason. He'd been perfecting his batter for centuries. He'd also perfected that twinkle-in-his-eye good boy look and he brandished the whole caboodle on Tiff.

Another elbow broke the spell. "What dragged your sorry ass out from the kitchen?"

"You. Or, more accurately, the lovely Tiffany." He smiled her way and she returned it, easily. Readily. "I had to see what made you stray from your usual order."

The bastard was messing with me. He knew I was under cover at Hagen. And he knew from Tiff's scent, she wasn't one of us.

No way could I have ordered my usual without revealing myself to her.

"It was all Tiffany's choosing." I squeezed her hand. She didn't squeeze back.

"You chose well." Jet tapped the menu in the little menu-holder thing on the table. "Two out of my three favorites.

She dipped her head, shooting the bastard a smile that made me want to deck his sorry ass. "Only two? Which missed the mark?"

"*Dark Knight*. It's been on the menu for longer than I can remember, and every time I try to spice it up, I get a backlash from my regulars."

I grinned. "Why mess with perfection?"

"Why, indeed?"

A yelp sounded from beyond the solid keypad-locked "staff only" door. Dana and Sally acting up to relieve the boredom in the second, more private section of the café. Their antics were as routine as my bi-weekly visits and my blood cocktail order.

Jet pushed up. "That's my cue." He reached across the table and Tiff twisted free of my grasp to entwine her fingers with his. "Lovely to meet you, Tiffany."

"Likewise."

"Come back again. Next time I'll prepare a special *Breakfast at Tiffany's* pancake just for you."

"Sounds tempting."

"That's the idea." He grinned, a dimpled, pussy-drenching grin he reserved for the ladies.

A screech followed by a clatter hijacked our attention. Jet's expression made me spare a brief thought for the two women. An angry head chef—particularly this one—was less than a pretty sight.

Yet, I couldn't say I was anything but glad to see him go.

His fingers flew over the keypad and we both watched as the door slammed at his back.

More clattering punctuated the low murmur of conversation around us. A siren wailed outside and a child began to cry. Much as Jet's arrival had called an end to Tiff's teasing, it had also shattered the ease in our conversation. Silence stretched between us.

Tiff twirled her fork, contemplating the remains of our meal. "He seems nice."

"More importantly, his pancakes are unrivaled."

"No disagreement here." She underlined the statement with a mouthful of berries and cream.

I attacked the last of the popcorn and salted caramel. With my dick no longer hogging the blood flow, my brain was once again operating full-throttle.

"Speaking of movies." We weren't, but it was a good opener to get us back on track. "Want to know what makes a great movie?" I tapped my fork on the plate and snagged a couple more popcorn. "Great actors like John Wayne, Clint Eastwood and Marlon Brando." I popped the fork in my mouth. "And if we're talking twentieth century, a little intrigue and a killer twist. Like *The Usual Suspects*."

"Twists are good. Predictable bores the shit out of me."

I nodded. "I'll second that. No action movies on your list?"

"*Atomic Blonde*. She's totally kick-ass, with a strength and sass I always envied."

"Why?" I covered her hand with mine. "You're strong and kick-ass. And don't get me started on your sass."

"People only see what we want them to see." Her gaze shuttered, as if my comment had flipped a switch.

"What does that mean?"

She pulled her hand free, avoiding my gaze. "Nothing. I am who I am. That's it." Her hand dropped beneath the table, and this time there was no mistake. Her palm rode my cock as if it were a travelator. "And what I am right now is horny."

15

TIFFANY

Gideon stalled my hand. "Don't think I don't get what you're doing. Every time conversation gets personal, you hit 'divert' with a come-on."

Damn. He was on to me.

I hated that. Most men couldn't read me, they were just glad for the whole sex-no-strings scenario. What guy didn't want that, for fuck's sake?

I speared him with my best take-no-shit stare. "And that's a problem, how?"

"What about the whole 'no sex' thing?"

He slid along the seat, breaking all contact. Not quite the reaction I'd been looking for.

I licked my lips, a tactic which always saw his gaze darken. "I changed my mind."

"Why?"

"Does it matter?"

He studied me beneath hooded lids. "Yeah, it kinda does."

He was exasperating the shit out of me. If he wasn't so

goddam good in the sack, I would have hightailed my ass out of there way before now.

I huffed. "I'm horny and you're here. Do we need a deeper meaning than that?"

Something cracked in his expression. I closed my mind to what that crack might signify. We shared nothing past sex. Dinner was a mistake, but we could rectify that—with more sex.

"What about the fact that I like you? Where does that factor in?"

A door closed in my brain. A big, double-bolted, steel-reinforced door. Anything outside sex required emotions and emotions hurt. I didn't want to hurt again.

"It doesn't." I inhaled. *Deep.* "I don't do relationships, and I definitely don't do *liking*," I air quoted, to make sure he got the point, "or all that emotional bullshit. What I do is sex, and I'm good at it. Turns out, you're pretty good at it too. I figure we may as well be good at it together."

He shook his head, as if admonishing a naughty kid. "No bullshit swings both ways, so here goes. I want more, Tiff."

"I don't do more."

"Why?"

"Stop asking me why and just accept that's the way things are."

"What if I say no?"

"Then I'll say we're done."

"No bullshit?"

"No bullshit."

Still, he kept his distance, his gaze locked with mine, as if by doing so he could delve deep into my soul and see . . . what? I turned away, breaking whatever voodoo magic he was trying to weave.

Why did everything have to be so fucking complicated?

More sucked. *More* meant complications and problems and all that bullshit I never wanted.

More meant one day things would turn to shit and I'd be less. *Worthless.* And a punching bag for the sonovabitch who convinced me that he wanted more and that *more* was good.

It was hell.

I didn't trust *more* any more than I trusted the man who spouted its virtues.

"And?"

"And?"

Would he stop repeating every goddam word I said and decide? I glared. Maybe looks were more effective than words.

He sighed. "Fine."

"Fine?"

"You want sex, no strings? Well, let's try it your way and see where that leads us."

"Just to be clear, it won't lead us anywhere but naked and fucking."

"We'll see." He had that smug "I'm in control" look on his face. The one he had that first day, when he walked into our meeting as if he owned it.

I didn't want smug, and I sure as hell didn't want anyone thinking he owned me. I didn't want him for any more than his cock. Time I made that clearer than mud.

"So, what are you waiting for? Shut up, take me out of here and fuck me, or forever hold your peace."

*T*here were few fantasies remaining in which I hadn't already indulged. One vaulted to mind with technicolor clarity as I wrapped my legs around Gideon's Harley and my arms tight around his chest—a sexy motorcycle, an even sexier man and multiple, mind-blowing orgasms.

Thankfully, I'd chosen my only ankle-length skirt with two side slits, allowing me to sit astride the bike with the barest semblance of modesty. A strip of fine silk lay between me and the leather seat, the cool air both teasing and tantalizing my pussy into hyperawareness.

I was throbbing and wet even before I sat on his bike, and it was a distinct possibility that the thrum of the engine and the heat of my thoughts would send me tumbling over the edge before we ever reached our destination.

He hadn't shared where we were headed. Then again, I hadn't asked. Talk had been pretty much nonexistent since I'd hit him with my ultimatum. Fine by me. I didn't want him for his scintillating conversational skills.

And I didn't want to lose the control I'd regained. That meant controlling the here and now and keeping Gideon off-kilter.

I tugged his jacket and yelled into his ear. "Turn here." His delectable body stiffened and I yelled again. "Turn. Left. Here. I know a place."

To his credit, he listened. He even turned, his shoulders so ramrod straight, the tension all but oozed into my numb fingertips.

"Next right."

The motorcycle dipped and we left the main highway for a gravel road. Five minutes and we'd arrive. My body hummed, so high from the promise of what was to come I could already feel the roll of an orgasm.

I squinted. Would I even spot the path? Bald Cypress lined the road and the motorcycle's headlights barely cut through the dark, winding road in front of us. Then the large information board glowed white in the hazy light and I knew we'd found it.

"Turn right just after the sign."

The path was narrow and barely discernable to those unaware of its existence. Perfect for what I had in mind. I spotted the large, gnarly oak, its heart-shaped knot sending shivers of not so delicious memories up my spine. I pushed them back. No time for that bullshit now.

"Stop."

The bike slid to a standstill, humming between my thighs. But now we'd arrived, it wasn't enough. I wanted Gideon there, fucking me into oblivion.

He cut the engine, engaged the stand and removed his helmet. I dismounted and did the same. The headlight cut through the dark until eventually swallowed by the night. The rush and bubble of the nearby brook cut through the quiet and rustling of the leaves above.

"Where are we?"

An owl announced his presence before swooping across our clearing from one tree to the next. "A place I come sometimes to think."

True. But I wouldn't tell him the rest.

He swung his leg up and off the bike, taking my helmet and setting it with his to hang from the handlebars.

"Why are we here?"

I shed my jacket. My breasts ached for his touch, my

nipples tight, hard buds, rasping against my top, driving me insane with want.

"To fulfil a fantasy." I popped the button of my skirt and slowly released the zipper. His gaze slid down to watch as the fabric puddled at my feet. I straddled the bike and leaned back against the storage compartment, lifting my leg, resting the arch of one foot on the gas tank. The other I rested on the ground.

I barely contemplated what would happen if the bike toppled over. Luckily, Gideon stepped forward, supporting the chassis.

I felt decadent. So fucking hot I could combust any moment.

I shed my top. No mean feat, but I made it without any major hiccups.

Gideon's gaze seemed riveted to my every move. My hands skimmed upward, from my knees, over my thighs, then beneath the soaked fabric to the throbbing folds beneath. I'd never considered myself an exhibitionist, but Gideon watching as my fingertips taunted the tight bud of nerves, his deep growl as I slowly entered my slick folds was the biggest turn-on, ever.

My free hand pulled the cups of my bra down, releasing my breasts, pushing them up and outward, freeing them to the cold night air.

Gideon swallowed, the bob of his Adam's apple drying my throat.

My gaze dropped from his almost black eyes to the unmistakable bulge in his jeans.

Fuck. Just thinking about his cock sliding inside, slow and thick, hard and deep . . . my breathing came faster, my fingers mimicking those actions.

"Take off your pants."

His gaze darted back to mine, his expression inscrutable in the muted light. His hands dropped from the bike to the belt at his waist. With excruciating slowness, he released the buckle, popped the button, then dragged open his fly. Black briefs enclosed his thick, aroused flesh and my mouth watered.

"I want to see you."

He barely hesitated before kicking off his boots, shedding his jeans and underwear.

"All of you."

His jacket slid off his shoulders and his biceps bulged with swoon-worthy splendor as he pulled his shirt forward and over his head.

"Come here."

He came, every fucking gorgeous inch of him, doing my bidding, making me so fucking crazy-hot I didn't know what I wanted most. I wanted to come, over and over, from my touch, from his, with his cock deep in my pussy, with his mouth sucking and fucking me till I couldn't remember my name or where the hell I was.

"Touch yourself."

That big, firm hand wrapped around his beautiful cock and he groaned. Not once did his gaze stray from mine.

Something splintered in my chest. Something unfathomable.

That rawness, that connection. It was too much.

I brought my fingers to my mouth and licked, tasting my arousal, watching his. Then slowly, I slid my hand back down to my throbbing flesh. His gaze followed its descent, accompanied by the rapid bob of his Adam's apple.

Much better.

"Pump and squeeze."

He did, sliding his hand balls to tip then straight back down again as I dipped two fingers then three into my wet-as-fuck pussy, imagining they were his, his mouth on my clit, his tongue entering me, twirling and sucking and fucking me halfway across the universe and back.

I felt the spiral, the heightening of my senses, the rush of my blood.

My body tensed, the edge of my climax so close I could taste it.

"I'm coming."

He didn't comment, just kept pumping, squeezing, sliding his hand up and down that delicious organ while I tumbled into orgasm, my pussy pulling and clenching my fingers as if they were his cock.

My hand slumped against my thigh, my body heavy and satisfied until my gaze lifted to Gideon's. He watched me, his massive body just inches from mine, his barely restrained control almost at breaking point.

I could see he wanted to touch me, to fuck me, and hell, I wanted that too.

Barely down from one orgasm, I was looking to the next.

I dragged my hand up over my hip, across my tummy, brushing and circling my breast as he watched, hungry, waiting for my command.

This massive, muscle-bound man, mine for the taking. Mine for the commanding. There was nothing on this planet more shit-hot than that.

16

GIDEON

"Taste me, Gideon."

Fuck.

I'd watched Tiff pleasure herself on my ride, wild, abandoned, sexy-as-all-hell. My balls were rocks, my cock so goddam hard it could obliterate boulders.

Yet, this was her fantasy and now it had become mine.

More than my next breath, more than my mortality and everything that went along with it, I wanted to taste her. My fangs threatened to descend and it took every ounce of my control to stop them.

She squeezed her nipples, two cherries beckoning for me to feast.

Until now, Tiff had commanded the show, but now it was my turn.

I stepped in and my fingers joined hers. She let her hand drop as I plumped her breasts, tweaking and twisting the taut buds until she writhed, bucking her hips, demanding fulfillment.

"Your mouth," she rasped. "I want your mouth."

That I could do. I took her lips, hard, uncompromising, groaning as they opened, allowing my tongue to plunder her sweet depths. Her tongue tangled with mine, her mouth giving and taking with unrestrained abandon.

Her hand wrapped around my cock and squeezed.

Fuck me.

Her thumb swept over the precum, slicking her palm before she squeezed again and worked my shaft like a stick shift in the frigging NASCAR series.

I broke the kiss. My hand squeezed her breast, my mouth sucking and swirling her nipple, harder and faster in response to her breathy moans. I reached between her thighs, slicking my thumb across her clit as I drove one, then two fingers into her pussy.

So. Fucking. Wet. So. Fucking. Hot.

I wanted inside her, to sink into her body and never come out.

Instead, I worked her clit, milking her pussy with my fingers, supporting the bike with my other hand, until she screamed my name.

"Fuck me. Gideon. *Please.*"

I didn't need a second invitation.

It took ten fumbled seconds to locate a condom in my jacket and roll it on.

I slid my hands up her thighs, helping her lift her legs to reveal her sexy ass and the slick, moist folds just begging for me to fuck them. I straddled the bike and she dropped her legs onto my shoulders, her passion-ridden gaze locking with mine.

I lowered her legs and dropped my mouth to her throat, to the hot, pulsing flow of blood just below the skin. I licked, sucked, tasting her. *So close.* Fulfilment beat less than an inch from my grasp. My cock throbbed just shy of her folds and I nudged closer, drawing on her throat, awakening my taste buds with the promise of satisfaction.

"Bite me!"

I stilled. Somewhere in the recesses of my mind I acknowledged what she wanted and how her command translated to me were eons apart, yet I couldn't stop.

My fangs descended, my nostrils drowning with her scent. Arousal. The life force rushing through her veins. I bucked, pushing into her with one swift motion, my fangs piercing her skin as I withdrew and thrust again.

Her gaze widened, her dilated pupils transforming her eyes to black. Short, sharp gasps escaped her parted lips, her hands frantically clutching my ass, pulling me in deeper, harder, faster.

The condom ensured we both experienced the connection without consummating the mating. Blood flowed across my tongue, awakening my taste buds, igniting my body. She tasted sweet, succulent, *alive*.

My balls clenched, so goddam tight, my cock so frigging hot, it burned like fire. I released her neck, licking the wound, thrusting harder, higher, building her orgasm as I stoked mine.

She moaned, mewled, panted, begged. I lifted her legs higher onto my shoulders, watching my cock enter and leave her pussy as my thumb flicked her clit, once, twice, circling and toying, making her arch and writhe and crazy.

One more flick and her nails cut into my ass. She screamed, pussy pulsing, pulling my cock into orgasm. I arched and unleashed, losing myself in the clench and grab of her flesh, leaving this world, this moment, my mind filled with everything and nothing all at once. Dark and light filled my vision, and *her*—blonde curls in disarray, cheeks cherry red, lips swollen and full.

Mine.

Possession billowed in my chest as if we'd mated and completed the ritual, when in reality we'd done all but the final, fundamental step—exchange essences, linking our souls to become one.

My cock was still buried deep in her body, my mind protesting over thoughts of breaking the bond. I dropped my forehead to hers, calming my breathing, relishing her uncontrolled panting and the rampant beat of her heart.

I felt peace and disquiet all at once.

And home.

I curved my palm around her jaw, brushing her cheek with my thumb. Our gazes locked, as tight as our bodies. Something brimmed in those hazy, blue depths—a fragility I'd never seen in her before now.

"Moja láska." I whispered the ancient words before I had the brain function to call them back.

Tiff blinked, and a shutter slid over her expression. She moved beneath me, wriggling, suddenly frantic to break free.

I pulled out and pushed up, bracing my thighs to keep the Harley from tumbling to the ground, searching her expression to glean what had suddenly changed. "You okay?"

She nodded, expression firmly closed. "Just a little cold." She shivered, as if to prove her point. More than "just cold" was responsible for obliterating her expression.

I shot her a grin. "I could warm you again."

Her palm connected with my chest, and at first I thought she'd pull me back down, but then she pushed and sat up. Her legs dropped down and I pulled my mind away from the sight of my motorcycle tucked tight between her thighs.

Her hand rubbed at her neck. "What the fuck just happened?"

I stood and stepped off the bike, gripping the handlebars, struggling for nonchalance. She scrambled off the seat, stumbling backwards in an effort to increase the distance between us. And here began the conversation I'd both anticipated and dreaded. "The best orgasm ever?"

That threw her, and I could see in her eyes it was true. I'd like to say modesty was one of my better qualities, but that'd be a lie. My ego swelled.

"What's this?" Trembling fingers pushed back her curls revealing the twin marks on her skin.

It was a discussion we needed, but not naked. I scouted around for my briefs. Luckily my better-than-mortal night vision located both them and her panties easily.

She'd already tucked her delicious breasts back into the lace that had only seconds ago plumped them up, ripe and ready for my enjoyment.

I dragged my thoughts away from that visual and back to the angry frown on Tiff's face. "You won't believe me if I tell you."

"Try me." The arch of her brows screamed "pull the other one," as if I were stringing her a line that was thin and tenuous at best. She'd soon discover I wasn't.

"Let's get dressed and go somewhere for you to warm up and I promise I'll tell you all." *Or almost all.* I ignored the twist in my gut. With more than our union at stake, there were some facts I had no authority to share.

"Just tell me."

"It's not that simple and you're cold." Her body shivered

again and I handed across her skirt, leaning in to help with her shirt buttons.

She pushed my hand away, her icy fingers fumbling to secure them.

I slipped into my jeans and shirt, holding out my jacket. "Here, take this."

"I don't need it." Her teeth began to chatter.

"Fuck it, Tiff. Stop being so goddam stubborn. Take the jacket before you catch the death of a cold."

I wrapped it round her body, ignoring the way she shrank away from my touch. It was impossible to equate this woman with the one who'd so brazenly ordered me to fuck her. I dropped the leather onto her shoulders and stepped back, relieved when she slipped her hands through the arms.

With jerky movements, she yanked up the zipper. "You're not the boss of me."

"You're right. But I do care about you. Would it surprise you so much that I don't want you to get sick?"

She opened her mouth then clamped it. She didn't have to voice the denial, it was written all over her face.

What the hell had happened between her need for me, her orgasm and this moment? Something had changed, some flick of a switch making her glare at me like I was the devil. Not a great start to a conversation that would see her view of me forever changed.

I handed her a helmet.

She took it, holding it away from her body as if it were infectious. "Where are we going?"

"Somewhere warm."

Uncertainty laced her expression. Damn, the woman could fuck me but she still didn't trust me. That she had good reason—considering I'd just bitten her without giving her the all-important heads up that I was a vamp—didn't factor. And I wasn't even going near the fact that I'd used her to access the flu antidote and cure.

It curdled my stomach. But the bite of conscience didn't absolve me of my sins. I was guilty as all hell, and I could only hope Tiff would be more forgiving than I'd be of myself before this whole sordid mess was over.

I straddled my bike. "Hop on."

Again, that uncertainty, before she dragged her feet and joined me, without actually joining me. Inches separated us.

"You'll have to hold on."

I waited, hating the distance between us, knowing the void would only grow once she discovered the truth.

Slowly her arms wrapped round my torso and I started the engine.

All I could hope is that in time, she'd find it in her heart to accept me.

17

TIFFANY

*F*uck.

My mind was a whirling dervish caught in a hurricane.

What the hell just happened?

I needed space. Distance. Time to process.

I gripped onto Gideon's waist, wondering how the hell I could have lost all sense of control so quick.

My fantasy had been going so well. I'd controlled the play, Gideon following my bidding without question or comment.

Hot. So fucking inferno hot.

I'd been burning, fueled by desire and the knowledge that he was mine for the taking. He'd stripped and my mouth had dried like a leaf in the summer heat. He'd touched himself, stroked and squeezed.

Fuck. I could have watched and come, just from the glorious sight of him.

Then he'd touched me and all thoughts had fled. I'd wanted him, his touch everywhere, his hands, his mouth, his cock. I'd even wondered if fucking could be more than a one-time thing between us.

He'd found that spot, that nervous center where shoulder and neck collide, and I'd gone wild. Ordered him to bite.

That was the moment.

He'd sunk his teeth into my skin, his cock into my flesh, and my mind had blanked. The light behind my eyes had flickered then come to life. I'd seen . . . *something*. What the fuck had I seen?

My desires? My future? An alternative, dream-worthy reality?

The vision—I had no idea what else to call it—had looked nothing like my life now and everything like the one I'd craved before I knew better.

In the throes of passion, I'd discounted it as part of the fantasy, but now, with the return of post-orgasmic clarity, I wasn't so sure. The images had seemed so real, so accessible. As if I could have reached out my hand and scooped them all up.

Gideon's bite had ignited something, something surprising, something surreal. And with hints of another life burned into my retinas, I couldn't wipe the possibilities from my mind.

I needed to get the hell away from him and fix what he'd broken. But first, I had to find out what the fuck he'd done.

Every inch of my body burned. And whereas before the burning had been bliss-related, now it was an itch that no amount of scratching could relieve.

The bike slowed and stopped.

A sensor light flicked on and I looked up to see an old, red-brick duplex. "Where are we?"

"Home."

I froze. "I'm not going in there."

"It's just to talk, Tiff."

"I don't care if it's to play tiddly winks, I'm not going in."

He sighed. "You want answers and what I have to say needs to be said in private. It's cold and dark out here, and I could do with a drink."

He shed his helmet, waiting.

TSTL flared in my mind in bright flashing neon.

Stupid bitch.

Fuck. When would that damnable voice forever leave my thoughts?

I stared at Gideon's square as square shoulders, still waiting, still patient. With as much dignity as I could muster, I held my skirt in place and dismounted the bike. He watched me, his expression so sincere, so open and guileless. He'd been nothing but honest till now. Could my trust stretch past dinner to frank conversation?

My gut said yes. But my gut had been wrong so many times before.

But not with Gideon.

Ping-pong thoughts battered my brain. I could trust him. But I didn't know him. But how much did you know anyone?

Gideon fucking Fang. The man was making me crazy.

I needed to know why.

I swallowed and prayed this moment wouldn't add to my pile of already overflowing regrets. "You have five minutes."

"I'll need ten."

I huffed. "Fine. Ten."

He nodded, dismounting his bike, leading the way up the cobblestone path. I blocked all thoughts of serial killers and rapists and madmen as I followed. Then we were standing on his rubber doormat.

He tapped a keypad and pushed open the door, standing aside for me to enter first. If nothing else, his manners had always been impeccable. Like any respectable serial killer.

He closed it behind us and my body jolted with the *click*. His ever-seeing gaze narrowed and I stepped back until I smacked into the wall.

His hand returned to the door. "This locking mechanism is pretty easy to open from the inside. If you need to leave at any time, just push this lever." He demonstrated and the door snapped easily open. His action warmed my still frosty body. He closed it again, and turned to me. "I'm making a drink. Want one?"

My instincts screamed "say no." "Sure."

I followed him through a hallway and down some stairs into an open plan living/dining/kitchen. Clean. White. Light. So not what I'd expected. Although, with Gideon, wasn't that the norm?

"Soy latte?"

"You have soy?"

"I do."

"Then a latte is fine." I hovered just shy of the kitchen, the click of my boots on his pristine tiles echoing loudly in my ears.

I'd given Gideon ten minutes, and demanded he tell me what he'd done. But now we'd entered normality—the bright lights of his kitchen—and left the craziness of the night behind, I wasn't sure what I wanted.

What kind of answer was I expecting?

I had a helluva hickey on my neck and a vision of happiness in my brain. Easy explanation—I'd had great sex and was still harboring fruitless dreams. Yet, there was something more. I couldn't explain it—how could I, when I didn't know what the fuck to explain—but something had happened the moment his teeth had connected with my skin.

I shivered, not wholly from cold.

I wasn't so sure I wanted to know what.

"Here."

"Thanks." I wrapped my fingers around the red ceramic mug. Maybe its warmth would go partway to abating the frost.

"Want to sit?"

Did I?

'Uh, no."

I stood beside the large, white-stone breakfast bar, with a clear run to the front door. Just in case.

He sipped from his mug and I sipped from mine.

Awkward.

I hated awkward almost as much as I hated more.

Time to rip off the band aid and deal with the consequences. "What happened back there?"

His mug froze midway to his mouth. A mouth that had pleasured me until I'd screamed his name. Multiple times.

Cut that thought. Multiple orgasms were the last place my mind should be wandering.

The skin on my neck was hot and tender and oh, so swollen. It didn't feel like a normal hickey, but then again, sex with Gideon hadn't felt like normal sex.

He lowered his mug and his riveting gold eyes captured my gaze. "I'm a vampire."

I snorted, spraying soy and coffee all over his pristine island counter. "Yeah, and I'm a werewolf." What kind of stupid-assed game was he playing? Anger accomplished what the drink hadn't. My blood boiled. "Seriously, Gideon? What the fuck? This isn't amateur hour on comedy night."

"I'd show you, but I don't want to scare you."

"Show me what?"

"How I pierced your skin."

He was deranged. He didn't seem deranged, but that only meant he'd learned to hide his madness behind a façade. I lowered my mug to the counter and measured the distance between myself and the hall.

"I won't stop you if you want to leave."

That he seemed to read my thoughts was more than a little unnerving. It only intensified my need to go.

"But before you go, I need you to understand who and what I am."

"Why does what I know matter?"

"Because I wasn't lying when I said I wanted you."

My stupid heart did a little flutter and flip, totally out of synch with my brain, which raged at his blatant manipulation. "For my blood?" It didn't hurt to play along. If Gideon thought he was a vampire, then far be it for me to burst his barbaric bubble.

"For you."

Okay, now my heart was full-on cartwheeling. "Don't do that."

"What?"

"Don't play me like that."

He scrubbed the back of his neck. "I'm not playing, Tiff. This is real."

Yeah, right. Vampire and all.

If he was throwing out fables instead of facts, I was wasting my time. I didn't need him to tell me I had an overactive imagination, I just needed out.

"You're a vampire. Good to know." I moved towards the entrance hall. "I should go now."

"You don't believe me."

It wasn't a question, more a statement. And one spoken with regret.

I grabbed my cell and with a couple of clicks, I ordered an Uber. I'd get out, go home and forget tonight ever happened.

"Sure, I believe you."

He shook his head and took one step, then another towards me. "Just remember, regardless of what you're about to see, I would never hurt you."

I backed towards the door. Something made me wary of turning my back.

Our gazes locked. Green eyes turned to gold, and as I watched, his skin blanched, his teeth slowly, gruesomely, beginning to grow. Sharp canines. Like a wolf.

Like a vampire.

Thunder roared against my eardrums.

I didn't wait for further explanations or to see more. I turned and ran. Not once did I look back.

18

GIDEON

For the first time in three centuries my lifeless blood chilled my soul.

I retracted my fangs and ran to the door.

I almost opened it. *Almost.*

My hand stalled on the cold handle. What more could I say? Tiff wasn't ready to hear how intrinsically we were bound and I wasn't ready to relive her distaste.

It cut. Like no other hurt, it cut like hell.

Her reaction was understandable. She'd just discovered a figment of her nightmares was real. And not only that, she'd had wild, mind-blowing sex with him.

I had no idea what to say to bring her down from that.

I turned and wandered aimlessly back towards the kitchen. I tossed the dregs of my coffee and contemplated making another. What was the point? It wasn't as if I could taste it or draw comfort from its aroma. Both were dead to me.

As dead as my aching heart.

That was a new one.

I needed to do something, but until I knew what, I was stuck in a turbine.

Mozart's symphony no. 5 pealed out from my pocket. I snatched out my cell. "*Tiff.*"

"Who?"

Not Tiff. Of course it wasn't. I was an idiot to think she'd contact me so soon.

"Damon."

"Gideon." He coughed, cleared his throat. "Who's Tiff?"

Something twisted in my chest. Not my heart. "A scientist at Hagen."

"That the same chick you took to Jet's?" Of course he'd heard. Rumors were like fodder when you had multiple lifetimes on your hands.

"Yeah."

"I heard you guys were pretty cozy."

"And?"

"Why shouldn't you get some on the side?"

It didn't sit well, letting Damon think Tiff was no more than a diversion. But first smell of more and he'd pull me out. Because the mission took priority, even over saving my soul.

The needs of the many . . . yada, yada, yada.

I knew I could balance both, but Damon would be harder to convince. My track record wasn't as shiny and unblemished as I'd like, regardless that the slip had been two centuries earlier. The man had the memory of a steel-reinforced lock box.

"Got any yet?"

An unfamiliar tightness clenched my chest. I'd never been one for fuck and tell. "Nah."

"Well, there's still time." I pictured his toothy smirk, the salacious light in his eyes. He still hadn't found his soulmate, but that didn't stop him from enjoying the entire female population while he searched. Some of us weren't so indifferent.

"That said, I'm sure I don't need to remind you, the mission comes first."

It was another dig, another reference to a time I'd allowed my emotions to rule my judgement. I'd since learned—through repeated, pertinent reminders—the error of my ways. But the bastard never let up. Back then, he'd become coven leader, gaining a stick up his ass and losing our friendship in the process.

I bit my tongue, once again swallowed apple pie with a side-serving of humble, and gave him what he wanted. "Of course."

I pictured his satisfied smirk. The satisfaction that once again he had me sitting up and begging with merely a word.

"How's things with the smelly scientist? Best buds yet?"

"Getting there. I'll be ready." I scrubbed the kinks from my neck and tipped my head left, then right. "Any news on d-day?"

"About a week. You'll need clear access to the antidote."

"I'll have it."

Silence yawned down the line.

"Don't fuck this up, Gid. Whoever this Tiff is, don't confuse which head takes precedence when the time comes. There's more at stake here than keeping your dick happy and your essence well fed."

With a click, Damon was gone. But I couldn't stop staring at my cell long after the call ended.

There had to be a way forward, to win Tiff and save the world. It sounded ridiculous—so superhero in spandex and tights—and frigging impossible. Any way I looked at it, I ended up screwing her and screwing us. And not in a good way.

That didn't stop me wanting to pursue her with every fiber of my being. Selfish? Yeah. I never said I was a saint. I'd searched for a way out my whole vampire life. Now I'd found it, I wasn't about to give up easy, regardless that it had happened now. Unease shivered along my spine. Call it bad timing or bad luck—the label didn't matter, the outcome was still the same.

I was about to betray the one person who could save me.

19

TIFFANY

*I*t had to be a prank.

If only.

Thoughts swirled, along with every bite of pancake that threatened to revisit if I didn't get my shit together.

I fucked a vampire.

The wind wailed, angry, unrelenting, whipping through my hair, fighting me every staggering step down his dark, semi-deserted street. A storm was brewing, an army of blustery clouds obliterating the sky, hacking away at any residual ambient warmth.

A dog howled from a nearby backyard. Shivers skittered down my spine, accompanied by visions of werewolves. Another imaginary being that shouldn't be allowed to escape the pages of fantasy fiction.

Was I losing my mind?

Vampires were myths. Legends. Creatures of nightmares, not earthbound and living in Louisiana. They didn't stampede into my life and seduce me into the best frigging sex ever.

I quickened my pace, pushing forward, increasing the distance between me and the lying sonofabitch.

He'd bitten me. A vampire bite. Did that mean I'd become one too?

Normal brain function became a thing of the past the moment I saw those teeth. The change in his expression. *Those eyes.* I hadn't stuck around to play show and tell.

The skin on my neck still felt hot and tender. More than a mosquito bite, considerably less than a snake.

I didn't *feel* different. Post-orgasmic bliss wasn't a precursor to vampirism, right? And I had no sudden desire to start drinking blood.

Why did that thought make me shudder, in a not wholly bad way? Had Gideon done that just now? Would I know if he had? Was that to blame for the intensity of my orgasm?

Expert Google was overdue for a consult. I'd check the moment I walked in my front door. Although what truth could Wikipedia and the entirety of the internet tell me when vampires weren't real?

Shivers rippled through my chest, mushrooming up and out to every part of my body. The air was frostbitten, but this chill gripped my insides, like gnarly roots gripped the earth that sustained them.

Gideon had promised no bullshit, then bullshitted me anyway.

Was I destined to become the physical or emotional punching bag of every blood-sucking bastard—pun so totally intended—in our fine and far-reaching United States?

Casual sex had stalled that slippery slope.

I stumbled. Pain ricocheted through my big toe as I froze, pebbles scattering out across the sidewalk and onto the road.

Clickity fuckity click.

My subconscious cowered in the dark recesses of my mind as a lightbulb flared. Was internal sabotage to blame for leaving me orgasmically challenged over the past three years? Had that super-controlling part of my brain influenced my partner choices and, ultimately, my disastrous sexual encounters?

Realization washed over me like a frigging monsoon.

If I'd been deliberately choosing the Peters and Pauls of this world, how the hell had Gideon made me break precedent? Did vampires have some voodoo superpowers to catch and captivate their victims?

Fuck.

Victim. There was a word I'd sworn to forever oust from my vocabulary.

How did he do it?

I was so fucking angry. At him. Myself. Both scrabbled for first footing. He'd ruined everything. Because how the hell could I revisit what we'd just done when he was . . . what he was?

Some higher power was lolling up in the clouds, laughing his fucking brains out. It was comedy hour in New Orleans. Dole out great—multiple—orgasms, then snatch them away.

Gideon fucking Fang.

A fucking vampire.

Stupid bitch.

This time, I had no choice but to agree.

20

GIDEON

The throwing room buzzed with hushed chatter and the intermittent crack of splintering wood followed the raucous whoop of success.

"Nice." Mannie waved his stubby hand towards the wooden bullseye showcasing my tomahawk dead center. "Must be beginner's luck."

I nodded, unwilling to share the fact that I'd handled an axe before now, in a time when it wasn't thrown for sport. "Money where your mouth is, Mannie. Best of three, loser buys the winner drinks."

"Better warm up your wallet, then. You're on."

I grinned. Spending time with Mannie wasn't as onerous as I'd first thought. He had a dry wit and a penchant for quirky hobbies, but we all had our quirks. And since he'd taken to using the salve I'd anonymously left on his desk, a formula courtesy of Dr. Weatherborne, an 1800s doc who had a thing for feet—*don't ask*—he wasn't smelling so badly, either.

As an added bonus, while I was throwing axes, I was less

absorbed in my funk over Tiff and her dogged determination to avoid me.

Mannie squinted towards the target, placing his right foot forward, raising his arms and axe over his head.

Twenty-four hours had passed since she'd run and I'd been unable to confront her for the chance to explain. She needed time, I got that. But time was one thing I didn't have. In a week my mission would be over, and after . . . who knew where Damon would place me? Doubtful I'd remain at Hagan much past that.

"Bullseye!" He broke into something that resembled a shuffle crossed with a moonwalk, far removed from the taciturn scientist I'd first met two weeks ago.

"Let's see how far first timer luck takes you."

I grabbed my axe, stepped up to the mark and focused. The target sharpened in my vision. I raised my arms over my head, aimed and threw.

The tomahawk landed exactly where I'd intended.

Mannie eyed the blade, lodged just inside the outer circle, unable to stem his grin, no matter how much he tried to mask it. "Better luck next time, Gideon." He slapped my back, much like a mother slaps a baby with gas. "Remember to extend your arms and . . ."

I zoned, inserting an intermittent nod when his voice waned. My mind seemed unable to accept that my chances for mortality were forever lost.

How the fuck could I win Tiff over? There had to be a way to slip back into her world. If I could get her to listen, I could explain away the whole vampire scenario and we could move past it and onto better pastures. Mortal, life-changing pastures.

"Your wallet's about to get a workout." Mannie poised, aimed, then tossed, his axe striking just shy of the bullseye.

I slapped his back and grinned. "Five out of five. That's a definite call for a drink."

"You got it." He recovered his axe and meticulously placed it in its case. Yep, the man had his own axe. If he wasn't such a teddy bear he'd have "serial killer" stamped all over his forehead.

"I was going to ask Jane if she'd accompany me to the lab's Christmas party. Or is that ridiculous, considering she'll be there anyway?" He grabbed his jacket and the case and we headed for reception. "What do you think?"

He looked at me as if I were the oracle on women, when in reality I hadn't a fucking clue. Story of my life. For his, the answer was much simpler.

"I say go for it, man." I matched my step to his slower, rambling pace. "There's a company Christmas party?"

He nodded. "Care of Tiffany, planning committee of one."

My ears perked up and my mind jumped feet-first into the root of an idea. "She doesn't have help?"

"She never asks. And no one ever offers. She seems to like planning, so we all leave her to it."

Interesting.

"Well, definitely ask Jane. But why wait? Why not invite her out for a coffee next week?"

"You think?"

"Yeah. What's the worst that can happen?"

His grip on the case tightened. "She says 'no.'"

"At least you'll know either way though, right?" Then he could move on and find someone else who returned his interest. At least he had that luxury.

A plan was forming. A win-win, of sorts, depending on how you viewed it. Hopefully Tiff would come to see it my way—after her initial shock and rage, that is.

I returned my tomahawk to reception and we stepped out into blustery cold, which made not a dent in my body temp. That didn't stop me from mirroring Mannie's braced, bent-over frame as we made for the parking lot and his cranberry-red 1959 Chevy El Camino—a passion only second to his axe throwing obsession.

Once he'd secured his gear in the cargo bed, he joined me in the cab. Hands braced on the steering wheel, he turned his deep-set brown gaze my way. "Where to?"

"Winner's choice."

He grinned. "I know just the place." He eased the stick shift into gear. The engine purred and Carly Simon blared out of the CD player, calling anyone listening on their vanity.

I lowered the volume. "How's work on the Flu A antidote?"

"We're almost a go." His shoulders swelled, so much so, I pictured his metaphorical feathers puffing up. "The intravenous serum is ready. We're just perfecting the aerosolization process so it doesn't reduce the antidote's potency."

"Interesting." Great news I could pass onto Damon. And maybe the fact I was delivering would see him ease up on his constant "don't fuck up" monologues. "I heard work is in progress to identify additional genetic mutations to ready the attenuated virus for airborne transmission."

He stopped at a red light and glanced over, clearly impressed. "You've done your homework."

"I find the whole process fascinating."

The light turned green and he eased back onto the clutch, shooting me a calculated look. "It's not yet common knowledge, but when this project is over, I'm moving to WHO. You should apply for my position in CDC."

"Congratulations." His news wasn't news, I'd already heard it from Graeme. What I found interesting was his offer for me to apply when Tiff should have had first dibs. No wonder she'd all but given up on my position. "Which division are you moving to?"

"Vector Control."

"Mosquitos, right?"

"Partially. Pretty much any living entity that carries and transmits disease." He spared me a glance. "Did you know that around seventeen percent of the estimated global communicable diseases are transmitted through vectors? Control the carrier and control of the disease will follow. That means . . ."

Again I zoned.

Large, fat raindrops splattered across the windshield, pelting down from a sky thick with angry gray clouds. Mannie leaned forwards to see beyond the *swish* of the wipers. Not that focus on the road affected his ability to speak.

I had other more pressing matters to occupy my thoughts. Like Tiffany, and how I was about to enter her orbit once again.

21

TIFFANY

*G*oogle didn't provide any damn answers.

"A vampire is a being from folklore . . ."

The author of that entry hadn't met Gideon.

There were a couple of entries about wannabes, cult followers who filed their canines into fangs and drank animal blood.

To each their own.

I scrolled through pages of unhelpful mythology—savage, blood-thirsty drawings and descriptions that looked and sounded nothing like Gideon—until I reached the bottom of page three.

Real life vampires. Creatures living amongst us in close-knit, closed communities.

Icicles spiraled through my blood.

Information was speculative, sketchy at best. Scant paragraphs outlining how "the condition" manifested in individuals post-puberty, random, with no known reason or cure. They lived amongst us, harmonious, well hidden. Could be a neighbor. A friend. A lover.

My heartbeat stumbled. I read on. *Some vampires practice the art of tantric feeding, extracting blood and energy through sexual encounters. These occurrences are highly charged and erotic, strengthening and revitalizing the vampire while providing their partners with a wholly satisfying sexual experience, most stating their orgasms to be unprecedented. For this reason, most vampires rarely lack for sexual partners.*

I was suddenly overcome with a strong need to shower. To scrub the memory of Gideon's touch from my skin and his cock from my body.

Seems I'd been relegated to some random source of energy.

I shut the screen. I'd seen enough.

If Expert Google was to be believed, my vampire bite would heal in a few days and I wouldn't transform into Count Dracula. Then again, EG had also stated that vampires didn't take unwilling participants. I may have been willing, but I wasn't informed. I'm not sure that still relegated me into the *willing participant* category.

Gideon had a helluva lot of explaining to do.

Thoughts of seeing him again shivered across my skin, raising the hairs at the back of my neck. A reaction not solely born of distaste. I hated that my body still craved his, even while knowing what he was. Was it sick that some perverted part of me found the idea of a revisit sexy? *That bite.* I'd not only seen something, I'd felt it. Like a current, surging through my blood, awakening my body, my each and every sense into hyperawareness.

My mind protested.

Regardless of who and what Gideon was, he represented

the kind of man I'd sworn never to allow past my hard-won control.

A liar.

Deception. Untruths. Little white lies that seemed harmless at first. They were the key to a Pandora's Box of harm. Because, with insincerity came uncaring, and what followed could only lead to hurt and heartache.

He'd used me to regain energy and strength. That I'd orgasmed was incidental. He'd still used me. And if he'd done it once, what was to stop him deceiving me and using me again?

"*A*h, Tiffany, do you have a moment?" Graeme shuffled papers at the head of the conference room table while everyone but the one person I wanted to avoid meandered out of the room.

Another weekly strategy meeting over. I'd successfully avoided Gideon since his Dr. Phil-worthy "I'm a vampire" revelation—even found a seat as far away from him and his new best bud Mannie as possible—but Graeme's rhetorical question looked to end my two-day hiatus.

"Gideon's graciously volunteered to help with the company Christmas party." My still clueless boss beamed, as if offering me roses instead of a whole new reason for my head to pound. "We're only a month out so I'm sure you'll be grateful for the help." The beam widened, making the Cheshire cat look positively sheepish. Something Gideon should have looked.

As if.

He hid his feelings behind a mask of bland indifference.

That didn't fool me. His ploy to get close to me once again was as obvious as the bite marks on my still tender skin. Just as well, the cooler temperatures made my turtleneck less conspicuous.

"That's not necessary. I'm all done."

He waved away my response as if swatting at a bug. "Gideon has a few ideas to spice the party up. I'm sure you can work together to give this year a fantastic send-off." Again he grinned. I'd never wanted to slap that diabolical look off his face more.

Steam surged through my body, pressure building in my skull, pounding smack between my eyes. I'd never volunteered to be events coordinator—I'd never been given the choice. The role had naturally fallen to me as the sole remaining female scientist on staff. Sexist, much?

Still, it beat remaining within range of Richard's ever-reaching tentacles. And until now, I'd successfully planned Christmas functions sans complaint. Until Gideon fucking Fang. Master graduate of Menace 101.

It was a *fait accompli*. The grit in Graeme's expression brooked no argument. I was stuck with Count Gideon, but that didn't mean I had to make his whole *getting back in my space* attempts easy. "Great. I'll send you a copy of my notes and we can work from there."

"Why don't we discuss it over dinner? Tonight."

Graeme slapped the rogue's back, nodding like some dreadful dashboard Elvis. "Fabulous. *Fabulous.*" He all but rubbed his chubby little hands. "The sooner you get together, the sooner everything will be finalized."

No point telling him it already *was* finalized. As usual, Graeme was totally clueless to my irritation and Gideon looked like he'd just won the war.

Not even close, buddy.

He was railroading me into his space and I wasn't having it. Gideon fucking Fang was about to discover I wasn't a pushover. He may have jumped into my pants—pretty easily, as it turned out—but he wasn't getting into my head. Or under my skin. And he definitely wasn't getting into my blood.

I shivered.

"I can't do dinner, but I can do drinks before. Let's say six-thirty, at Romeo's?"

He grinned, a cocky, all-knowing glint lacing his expression. *Bastard.* I knew exactly what he was thinking. We'd done coffee, we'd done dinner. Now we were doing drinks. What exactly that meant and where it sat on the "getting to know you scale" I neither knew nor cared. This was work, with a side dish of vampire show and tell. If I had no choice in the matter, the least I could do is use the time to my advantage.

And while I was at it, I'd let Gideon know categorically that he and his vampirish ways could—in the most mature manner possible—get stuffed.

22

GIDEON

G raeme was a clueless bastard. But at least his ignorance helped me snag the one thing that had eluded me since my disastrous vampire reveal— one-on-one time with Tiff.

I downed my first vodka and lime and raised a hand to order another, wishing I could feel its effects and dull the cut of her rejection.

The bar was full to near overflowing. We'd be hard-pressed to find a table, let alone space for two at the bar. Maybe that was her plan. Make it impossible for conversation of any kind, particularly of the personal nature.

She had to know I'd want to fix whatever my revelation had broken between us. And I imagined she'd dump every roadblock possible in my way. Well, as fast as she blocked, I'd unblock.

Awareness rippled up my spine. She stood just inside the doorway—dressed head-to-toe in black—seemingly oblivious of the crowd and patrons milling around. Her gaze fastened unwaveringly on me.

Any best defense was a good offense, and throwing Tiff off balance was the only way to retain even footing. I knocked back the remainder of my drink and cut through the crowd. "Something's come up. We have to go."

Her mouth opened, no doubt to protest, but I didn't wait to hear. Luckily her choice of venue wasn't far from my choice, so I led and she followed, with dragging feet and a frown so long it almost scraped the ground.

"Here." The blue-painted door gave no indication of what lurked behind it and Tiff's expression said she wasn't enthralled with finding out. I didn't give her time to reflect, just pushed the door and stepped aside for her to enter.

"Why are we here?"

"To show you something."

She eyed the dimly lit stairs warily.

"You'll enjoy this even more than the pancakes."

More wariness, only this time laced with a flood of scarlet to her cheeks. She had to be remembering our post-pancake activities. My body did the same, the memory filling and tightening my balls.

I ignored the grip of denim across my groin and focused on the angry line of her lips. "This way." I began climbing the stairs. She had two options, follow or leave. For once I didn't have a clue which she'd choose. I just placed one foot in front of the other and hoped it was the former.

The hesitant slap of her soles against the wood followed me and I couldn't help but smile. Here was my chance to fix things between us. My chance to make things right.

*W*e snagged a table towards the back. The floor was packed, but not so packed that Marcos couldn't wrangle a space for an old pal. He owed me, and despite never asking for payback, whenever I showed, he gave it to me anyway—a table and an endless stream of original cocktails. His specialty, but not the reason regulars flocked to *Blues on Tap*.

That—or rather, *he*—sat on the small, raised dais, making love to the strings of his Gibson—a gift from his old buddy, BB King. I'd never seen Jonnie without it. No surprise if he slept with the damn thing. The guy was a loon. His wife, Joelene, would warm a bed—and the man in it—better than any slab of wood. Even one carved from the highest quality mahogany.

She sat at her usual table, front row center, supporting the man she'd married over two centuries ago. They'd both lost their soulmates to tragedy and had since found comfort in each other's arms. Raven locks cascaded down Joelene's shoulders, her curvy figure painted into a shimmery silver number. Stunning.

Yet she didn't stir my blood like the woman whose icy, lance-tipped stare cut through the dim lighting across the table. "Want to explain why you railroaded me here?"

"Sure." I was fast running out of ways to smooth over her animosity. I grabbed the drinks menus from between the arms of a mini Eric Clapton and dropped one in front of her. "How's your seat?"

She leaned back in her chair and squinted. "O–kay."

"Like the music?"

She dipped her head. "I guess."

I grinned. "That's why."

"Romeo's was fine."

"Sure, if you want to stand shoulder-to-shoulder with strangers and lose your voice trying to be heard."

"One drink and I'm going. I don't need comfort and quiet for that."

It was like trudging uphill, through Jell-o, in one-size too big galoshes. "Doesn't mean you can't enjoy the ambiance. And Marcos makes killer cocktails, so if it's only one drink, we may as well make that one drink count."

"This isn't a date, Gideon."

"I know."

"I don't appreciate being railroaded into this whole help-me-with-the-party situation."

"I know."

"And I really hate the whole patronizing 'I know' commentary you have going."

"Yeah, I get that." I sighed. "We need to talk, Tiff. And not about the damn party."

She sighed, deep and slow, and I couldn't help but notice the rise and fall of her breasts, couldn't help remembering how perfectly they'd filled my palms, how their texture and taste had rendered life to my deadened taste buds. How I wanted to feel that life flow through me again.

"You're right. We do have to talk." She inhaled, deeply, and although I held my gaze eye-level, I still pictured the pull of her breasts against the fabric of her high-necked top. Still remembered the zap as my fangs punctured her skin and her essence flowed across my tongue.

"What the fuck, Gideon?"

I pulled my attention back to the fire in her eyes and shot her a grin. "Is that a question?"

"Is everything a fucking joke to you? You bit me, for fuck's sake. *Bit me*. You could have turned me into a fucking vampire."

"It doesn't work that way."

"So, tell me *how* it works. Tell me how you think fucking me without telling me what you are is okay."

Chatter dwindled around us and I felt the jab of each and every stare. "Want to lower your voice?"

"Why? The *ambiance* not loud enough for you now?"

The situation was spiraling from bad to ball-breaking. Tiff wasn't ready to listen, much as she'd asked me to explain.

I caught Margherite's gaze from across the bar. "We need a drink."

What I really needed was to avert the conversation before it ended in disaster. Before Tiff stormed off and I waved goodbye to all chances of mortality.

With expert precision, Margherite weaved through the tables, delivering the half a dozen or so cocktails from her tray as she made her way towards us. No need for her crystal ball skills—my frustration had to be plastered all over my face. "Hey, y'all."

Tiff twisted her lips into what could have been a smile, if the light had reached her eyes. "Hi."

Margh flicked a cascade of red curls over her shoulder. "What can I get to tantalize your taste buds?"

I turned to Tiff. "The Muddy Waters Mudcake is amazing."

She ran her finger slowly down the open page, her jaw clenched so tight it'd be a miracle if her teeth didn't shatter. "I'll have . . . the Stevie Ray Vaughan Slinger." She slapped closed the menu and dropped it back into Eric's arms.

"The Ma Rainey Red Berry Sling for me, thanks, M."

"Sure thing, Big G." She winked and smiled and sashayed back towards the bar.

Tiff's gaze swung from Margh to me. "Do you know every restaurant and bar owner in New Orleans."

"Not *every*." I cocked a brow in response to the arch in hers. "There are benefits to living over three hundred years."

Her jaw dropped. "You're three-hundred years old?"

"Three hundred and forty-seven, to be precise."

She dropped back into her chair, scanning my face, no doubt looking for some indication—lines, wrinkles, grey hairs—something to show my life had spanned centuries. She swallowed. "You don't look a day over two hundred."

Humor. It was an improvement on anger. I could work with that.

I stroked my chin. "Oil of Olay."

Lagoon blue eyes widened. "Really?"

"Nah." I shot her a grin she didn't return. But we were talking, and talking wasn't walking away and shutting me out. It was a win, of sorts.

And an opportunity to let her into my world.

"Vampires don't age." I sensed her focus. On me, not the world around us. "We're immortal, trapped at whatever age we turned. Mine was twenty-nine."

"When you were bitten?"

I shook my head. "When I fell prey to the genetic roll of the dice." I'd long since moved past the resentment, but that didn't mean my reality no longer cut. I shrugged, failing to loosen the clamp in my shoulders. "Fate's funny like that. It governs us all. Has the power to give love. Comfort. Happiness. An eternity of hell." I leaned forward. "Two percent of humans carry a vampire gene. There are no rules governing when it switches on, but when it does, a new vamp is born."

"Vampirism is genetic?" Her surprise was no different than most of us who'd turned and discovered the cause. The fucked-up consequence to having the right gene and the wrong goddam luck. "So, it's like eye color and sex?"

"Yeah. A rare, recessive gene, which sometimes activates, and sometimes lies in wait, passing through generations until someone in that line turns."

"Fuck."

A less vigorous sentiment than the one I'd uttered when I turned, but it wasn't far off.

She swallowed, as if her new knowledge had formed a swelling deep in her throat. "So everything I learned from Buffy is crap?"

"Not everything." I grinned. "There really *is* a Hellmouth in Cleveland."

"How can you joke about it?"

"What would you rather I do? I've had centuries to come to grips with my fate." I swallowed. "And centuries to find my way out of it."

Margh returned with our drinks. Great timing. I needed the cool liquid to soothe the burn in my throat.

Tiff watched Margh weave her way back to the bar, then she returned her attention to me. "There's a way out?"

"For some."

"How?"

"*Two marks make one, two hearts made whole. Love and essence combine, mortalizing the soul. Truth and honor abound, in this life and the next, mates of body and soul, the curse eternally vexed.*"

"What is it?"

"A prophesy. The recipe for my redemption." I searched for a reaction, something to indicate what she was thinking. I got nothing but an expression perfect for poker.

"The curse?"

"Madness and bloodlust."

"Mates of body and soul?"

"Soulmates."

I could see the cogs turning in her mind, the realization when it hit. "You're looking for your soulmate?"

"I found her." I caught her gaze, bottomless oceans of blue that could drown a soul if given free rein. She waited, unaware that complicated was the very least her life was about to become. "It's you."

23

TIFFANY

For once, no words came.

Soulmate to a vampire.

What the fuck?

It was some cruel joke. It had to be. More than him fucking me. More than his bite.

Our conversation had turned light. Frivolous. Like the raspberries that tangoed across my taste buds and the lime that tickled my throat.

I was still angry. At his duplicity. At the double puncture wounds still burning my neck.

But his words made me feel something more. Not so much sympathy, as understanding. I knew what it was to be a victim of fate. A victim, by the simple roll of the dice.

My father would not have been my father if my mother hadn't left the slopes of Val d'Isère for the distant isles of New Zealand. My life might have played out differently. Perhaps Richard and I would never have met.

Perhaps, I wouldn't have born the scars that saw me find and fuck Gideon.

Fate was a fucked-up motherfucker.

I knocked back the remains of my slinger, barely mindful of the tart berries, the burn of ginger as it lit a fire in my stomach.

My glass clattered against the scratched, over-scrubbed wood. I glanced at my watch and filled my lungs with much-needed oxygen. "I have to go."

"Can we talk about this?"

"What's left to say? You're a vampire, I'm your soulmate, and you want me to save you." I scrubbed my temple, but the pound inside didn't lessen. "Did I miss anything?"

"Plenty." He shook his head. Weary. Three-hundred plus years' worth of weary.

I braced my heartstrings against the tug of that thought. "Well, I know all I need to know."

"Please stay. You don't have all the facts, and once you leave, I lose my chance to explain."

"Tell me something. All this crap about wanting 'more,'" I did that whole air quote thing, "is because you believe I can save you, right? It's not about *me* or how you feel about *me*. It's all about you."

He hesitated, and that hesitation said it all.

My hand cut the air between us. "No bullshit. You promised."

He sighed. "Yes." He reached out for my hand, but I pulled it back before he could touch me and turn me with that touch. He dragged his hand back across the table and sighed. "How can it be about more if you don't let me in? I want to know you. I've tried to know you. How could I not, if you're the one I'm to spend the rest of my mortal life with?"

"How can I believe you when you've kept things—critical things—from me? Like the fairy-sized fact you're a frigging vampire, for fuck's sake."

"I did that because you weren't ready. If I'd revealed I was a vampire in the sterility room, how do you imagine that would have gone down?"

"I'd have relegated you to the looney bin."

"Right." He quirked a brow. "And now?"

"I'm relegating myself to the looney bin." I tipped my head, trying to see past the normal. Only, he was far from normal. A mere glance raced my heart, a mere touch heated my blood. A mere bite made me feel and see things beyond my wildest imagination. Yet, I couldn't look at him without the memory of those fangs. I shuddered. "You're not real."

"We both know that's not true."

"Not you. Vampires."

"I wish you were right, but unfortunately you're not."

The helplessness of his words flattened me beyond belief. "I don't know what to do with this."

"It's been more than three-hundred years since I turned, and I still don't know what to do with this. All I know is that fate has chosen you for me, and fate has brought us together now. It's up to us to figure out the rest." He reached across the table, the tips of his fingers stopping just shy of my hand. This time I didn't pull back. "Stay and have another drink. Let's talk. Pretend we're two random people getting to know one another."

"I have to go. I have plans."

"And we both know that's a lie." His green-gold gaze pierced mine. "No bullshit swings both ways, Tiff. Can we at least both pledge from this moment on for nothing but honesty between us?"

132

My mind whirled. There was no "us." There was just me, a mortal, and him, a vampire. He wanted forever and all I'd wanted was a simple, no-strings fuck.

This was totally fucked.

I was fucked.

Because I looked into his eyes and I wanted to believe. In two hearts becoming whole. In destiny. In something bigger and better than what I had now.

In the vision.

It was just a drink. Just conversation. Anything beyond that would be my choice.

What that meant for Gideon and his future, couldn't, wouldn't, factor.

I ignored the guilt. Guilt had led me to where I was now. Guilt over the implosion of my life, my family, my disastrous relationship with Richard. I'd vowed never to allow guilt to govern my decisions again. I wouldn't—couldn't—open myself up to the aftermath that invariably came. I'd survived once. No guarantee I'd survive next time round.

It was just a drink.

It wasn't a date.

It was a fact-finding mission to discover all I needed to know before I could make my decision and move on.

I crossed my arms, crossed my legs, crossed my heart, hope to die if I ever made the wrong decision again.

"Order me a Bessie Smith Breeze and tell me why you're so sure I'm the one."

*V*odka and cranberry tripped across my tongue.

I couldn't deny I was drawn to Gideon. I'd been drawn since the moment my eyes clapped on him. I'd believed it was sex—or the promise thereof—but what if it was more?

"You have a birthmark on your neck."

My fingertips brushed the familiar raised, slightly rough skin just shy of his bite. "And?"

"I have a mark the mirror image of yours."

"So?"

"Together our two broken hearts will become one."

Something clicked. "The Prophesy."

"Yes. The Prophesy."

"And the essence."

"That's our joining."

"You mean sex."

He nodded.

"And what about 'the curse eternally vexed' part?"

"Vampires are cursed, but not in the way you may think." He shot me a wry grin. "You mentioned Buffy before. Well, in simple terms, real vampires are more like Angel and less like Spike. They're sane, they're basically good, and they don't harm humans. That is, until 'The Change.'"

"The Change?"

"The vampire gene mutates, turning Angel into Spike. Turning good into evil." He tensed. "And once you turn, you can never change back."

It was like he'd dropped a ten ton weight on my shoulders. "So, if we don't 'bond?'"

"Sometime in my future, I become a monster. Mad. Bloodthirsty. A killer."

The words left his mouth, soft and low, but I heard them all the same. My blood chilled. What kind of a monster was I if I refused him? Knowing what I knew now. Could I condemn anyone—*him*—to an eternity of hell?

"So, explain why we've had sex, twice, and you weren't saved."

"It's not just about sex. The ceremony requires trust and commitment. I bite you and we make love, with no impediments."

"You mean no condoms."

"Yes."

"Why not just say that?"

"The Prophesy is ancient and it is what it is. The words, the intent, the effect. It was written in the blood of the first, to be upheld till the last."

"More prophesy?"

"There's an entire diatribe of it. I could spout you sayings until your head spins, but it all boils down to one thing—if a vampire fails to bond with their soulmate, they'll live forever lost in a haze of madness and bloodlust. That is, unless their coven finds them and performs a mercy killing."

The chill turned to frost. I shook my head, shaking that thought. Shaking the vision of a crazed, bloody Gideon, a stake piercing his non-beating heart.

Bile scoured my throat. The idea, the consequence of my decision, was too, too awful. How could I ever escape from it?

Yet, much as every word made me cringe, I had to know one more thing. "Tell me what it's like."

He leaned back in his seat—*sprawled*—watching me through hooded lids. "What what's like?"

"Life as a vampire."

He closed his eyes for just one second, then his gaze bored into mine. "Long. Lonely." He inhaled, long, slow, then exhaled on a hiss. "Immortality sounds great, until you realize what it means. Leaving your old friends and family for fear they'll discover what you are. Making vampire friends, knowing that one day The Change could tear them from your life. Living in fear of losing the last traces of your humanity as The Change comes for you."

Every word cut a little closer to my heart. I tried to smile, but the twist of my lips told me I'd failed abysmally. "So, nothing good."

"That's not completely true." He scrubbed the back of his neck. "Not everything was bad. I've formed a part of history. I've *been there*. The rise and fall of Napoleon. Mozart playing in Salzburg. Gold rushes. Inventions. The first flight. Man's first walk on the moon. Wars. Victories. Tragedies and triumphs. I've seen them all unfold, first hand." His gaze turned inward to another place, another time. "I shook hands with Martin Luther King. Rubbed shoulders with Abraham Lincoln. Shared a drink with JFK. I kissed Marilyn Monroe and debated physics with Marie Curie."

A tiny smile twitched his lips. "But I have to say, one of the highlights is being immortalized on television. Spot any resemblance?" I shook my head as he turned his face left then right. "One of Buffy's original screenwriters was a vamp and she tailored Angel's character around me." He grinned. "True story."

More jokes, when this situation was about as funny as a firefly caught in a web. The more they resisted, the more entrapped they became.

A sip of my drink. Another. Nothing helped clear the lump in my throat.

He watched me and more than anything, I wanted to hide. To escape from that all-seeing gaze.

His expression softened. "Enough about me." He sipped from his drink but never once let his gaze stray. "What was it like growing up in The Land of the Long White Cloud?"

Iron claws clamped my chest. Of all questions to ask, this was the one I'd never answer. And where before I'd distracted with sex, now I had to employ other diversions.

"Cold. I prefer the warmth of Louisiana."

"Do you still have family back home?"

"None that I know of." That much was true. My father had long since vanished and my mother . . . well, he'd seen to it that I never knew her past my fifteenth birthday. "I haven't been back to New Zealand since I was seventeen. This is my home now."

"Why Louisiana?"

"Why not?"

"You had fifty States to choose from, yet you chose this one. Surely, you have a reason."

"Why couldn't I just close my eyes and point at a map?"

"Who plans their life playing pin the tail?"

Me. But perhaps that revelation was more telling than I'd like. "No one." I topped up my empty glass from the water jug in the center of the table. "It seemed like a laid back place to live. Was I wrong?"

"No."

I wanted to shrink under his scrutiny. But that, too, would be telling. "We should discuss the party."

His brows dipped in a perfect V, playing innocent when he had to know what party.

"The party that sparked this dinner in the first place."

"Ahh, *that* party." Perfect lips slid into a perfect grin.

Something in me wanted to slap the perfection from his face. I dropped my fisted palm in my lap and shot him a tight smile. "I've planned the company's Christmas party for the past three years and never once had a complaint. What's this fabulous idea that'll undo all the work I've done so far?"

More grinning. My fist tightened. "A microbe masquerade ball."

GIDEON

S he'd accepted the news of my vampirism better than she'd accepted my suggestion for the party. *Accept* being a very loose, very relative term.

Who knew my soulmate was a control freak?

Soulmate.

The word had a warm, coffee-rich ring, where before it had worn uncertainty.

It felt good to finally be open with Tiff. To share my life in a way I hadn't for centuries. That there were still parts of me I couldn't share—my mission for the coven just one biggie—was a niggle in my gut I'd just have to bear. In a week it would be over and incidental. And if things went well, I'd be mortal and able to leave all the deceptions and untruths behind.

"I think we're done here." She pushed back her glass and clutched her purse in both hands. "I'll redesign the invites and you can reorder the canapes and cocktails. The venue won't change, but we'll need to rethink the decorations."

Yep, control freak.

I kinda liked it. Tiff, all busy and business-like. All buttoned up and staid, just waiting for me to unbutton and rumple her into ecstasy. My balls tightened with the thought.

Much as I stood more chance of flying and brandishing a red cape, it didn't hurt for a vamp to try. "Why don't we discuss the decorations tomorrow? Over dinner?"

"Emails will work fine."

"But they're not half as much fun."

She sighed. "I need time to process this, Gideon. Don't rush me."

I looked at her then. Really looked. Her skin lacked its usual color, deep lines carving beneath her eyes and across her brow.

I was a selfish bastard.

In my defense, I'd waded through centuries to find her and now that she'd appeared, I wanted everything The Prophesy promised—*mortal of body, seed sown of the soul and purity of line continued.* And I wanted it yesterday.

I wanted a normalcy so simple, so white-picket-fence and all, to wipe the past three-hundred years of hell from my memory. And Tiff was the one to do it.

If she needed time, I had no choice but to give it.

"You're right." I stood, taking her jacket from the back of her chair and holding it open for her. "I'll take you home."

She slipped her arms in, keeping her distance, pulling away to avoid my touch. I won't pretend it didn't cut.

"I can walk."

"I know. I've seen you do it." I shot her a wry grin. "But it's late and dark and the streets aren't safe. Let me do this for you."

First instincts would have seen her refuse. Then she

glanced out the window and saw what I saw—wind lashing about the mass of trees lining Ol' Man River.

She nodded, and inwardly I sighed.

My motive was two-fold—I'd see her safely home, but first I'd enjoy the wrap of her body around mine. Just one advantage of owning a motorcycle, of which there were many.

Visions of her decadent body splayed across the leather and chrome had me hard immediately.

That encounter wouldn't be our last. It couldn't be. Not with the promise of mortality within reach. Not while Tiff held my future—our combined, transformed future—in the palm of her tightly clenched hand.

he moment we arrived at her apartment building, she pulled away and all but leapt off the bike. She shed her helmet and held it out for me to take. "Thanks."

I kicked back the stand and dismounted, disposing of both helmets. "I'll walk you up."

"No need."

"I know. But I'll do it anyway." I touched her shoulder, just a touch, to stop her walking away. "I don't remember much about my mother, but I remember enough to know she'd have a fit if I didn't see a lady to her door."

She shrugged free of my hand, but she didn't leave. "What was she like?"

The hollow around my heart wrenched. My memories of back then were hazy—warm happiness followed by years of loneliness and regrets. "I don't remember much. She smiled often. Made Dad and me laugh a lot. We had fun together."

She looked to the passing cars in the distance, her gaze drawn inward. "My mother rarely smiled."

I tried to remain calm. Tried to act as if her finally sharing a part of her past wasn't the biggest event since Shin-Soo Choo joined the Texas Rangers. "Even now?"

She pulled back her gaze. "Especially now. She's dead." She clamped her lips then, as if the words had escaped despite her need to keep them hidden.

I took her icy hand in mine and squeezed. My cold skin may not warm her, but I could only hope the gesture would. "I'm sorry."

She nodded. A sharp acknowledgement, nothing more, and tugged her hand free, shoving both into her jacket pockets.

I let my hand drop. "When did she die?"

"I was fifteen." She swallowed. Took a deep breath. "What about your mom?"

Memory evoked a pair of blue-grey eyes and a soft, lilting voice. Imagination filled in the rest. "She lived to be forty-nine. A good age back in the 1700s." My lips twisted. "I hate to think that my disappearance wiped the smile forever from her face."

"You just disappeared?"

"What other choice did I have?" I scrubbed my neck. If only I could scrub out the kinks, every last, regretful one. "Back then, immortality was labeled a sign of the devil. They'd have rammed a stake through my heart then burned my body until there was nothing left." I shuddered, the reality of that death not solely relegated to the past if I couldn't fulfil The Prophesy and avert The Change. "Think about the number of missing persons who are never found. Where do you think they go?"

"You mean they're all vampires?"

"Not all, but it wouldn't be far off ninety-nine percent."

The bag in her hand shook. "That accountant in the French Quarter?"

I nodded. "And the couple out near City Park."

Her wide, liquid gaze blinked. "Fuck."

She was slowly coming to grips with my world. It wasn't pretty. Her mind had to be spinning, a crazy "free me from this roller coaster" spinning.

Her palm dropped to my chest, to my cold, unbeating heart. "I'm sorry that happened to you."

"Yeah. Me too. But if it hadn't, we would never have met. That's a definite upside for me." I covered her hand with mine, pushing my lips into a smile. "Some folks spend their entire lives searching for their soulmate, seeking to fulfil their destiny, only to fail because the other half of their soul belongs to a different time. We're lucky. We span centuries, yet our search is over."

Her expression said she didn't share my sentiments. How could she, when she'd been bombarded with information I'd had ten lifetimes to process?

She needed time.

She shivered.

And she needed out of the cold.

"Let's get you inside. It's freezing out here."

She stared at me, questioning. "Is it?"

"For you, yes."

"But not for you."

A familiar boulder weighted my chest. "How can you feel cold when your blood runs like the dead?"

"I can't imagine what that must be like."

"And I hope you never have to." My palm dropped to her

back, guiding her towards the winding path leading to the complex's front door. She walked, and I stayed at her side, my palm still at her back.

The night swallowed the grounds, the street lamps that would have lit our way long since smashed. It wasn't uncommon in this part of town. Regardless of the dark, my vamp vision could see what the human eye missed.

A shadow, flesh and bones, pushed away from a large maple to our right.

I pulled Tiff behind me and stepped forwards. I sensed her stiffen, her tremble. I smelled her fear.

"Richard?"

She knew the shadow?

"Tiffany?" The fuckwit mimicked her strangled whisper.

I took another step forward. "What do you want?"

"To talk to an old friend."

Tiffany shuddered.

I pushed up taller, flexing my muscles. "She doesn't want to talk to you."

He sidestepped. "You got this joker speaking for you? Does he sit and play dead as well?"

I stalked forwards. Her hand grasped my elbow, trembling but firm. She shook her head, and much as I hated it, I held back.

"What do you want, Richard?"

"Can't I stop by and see how you're doing?"

"Washington is far from a stopping by scenario, so, no." She inhaled. "We're over. We've been over for three years now. You need to stop stopping by."

"It's a free world."

"So, go explore it. Move on. Find someone who wants you in her life."

"You've grown balls since I last saw you. Are they his?" The prick tipped his head in my direction. I tensed, but Tiff's grip tightened so I stayed put.

"That's none of your business."

"It is if it interferes with your job."

"I don't work for you."

"Think again, sweet pea." His nostrils flared, like a bull seconds before a charge. "You'll hear the announcement soon enough, but let me share the highlights. The Pax Group is about to take over Hagen Pharmaceuticals. That means you and me, together again." The prick sneered. He had big, fucking balls, all right, and I wanted to rip them from his body and feed them piecemeal to the gators.

I had no idea what this douche meant to Tiff, or what history they shared. I did know that her grip was so tight, her nails dug deep into my skin.

The time for holding back had long past. I stalked towards the dumbass and flexed my fists. "Fuck off before I do something you'll regret."

"Hey, man, no need to get your nuts in a knot. I'm gone." He rolled his hand through the air. "See you round the office real soon, sweet pea."

He sauntered off, a bull who'd bested the matador and knew it.

"What the hell was that about?"

Now the prick was gone, she pulled her hand back. "Nothing."

"No bullshit, Tiff. That asshole had an agenda, and it was intimidation. What I want to know is why."

She drew in a breath, closed her eyes for just one second, then focused on my left ear. "We went out, he hit me one too many times and now we're done. Only Richard doesn't do no." Her shoulders sagged, as if hit once again. "And now he's part of Hagen's, I need a new job."

*The hours dragged.

I filled them with work and mindlessness and man-bonding with Mannie. Hollow, flavorless moments unfolding before me like a recipe minus ingredients. Nothing enriched the time like Tiff. Her wit. Her smile. Even her disapproval. I missed them all.

I even succumbed to Netflix. Endless, mind-numbing episodes with no real purpose other than to fill hours waiting for a decision. For an end to my uncertainty.

My mind circled then recycled our last meeting. How she'd opened up about her mother. How Richard's actions had provided insight into her disdain for men.

So much made sense now. I understood her need to remain distant and hold her emotions in check. Her need for control. It was the reason I'd respected her wishes and taken a step back. The reason I watched the roll of a TV series now when I hadn't a clue what was happening.

Mindless.

A loud knock echoed from the vicinity of my front door. Strange, when I had a doorbell in perfect working order.

The security camera was no use. Whoever stood on my doorstep remained hunched beneath an oversized black coat and hood.

No matter who had knocked, they offered a break from my monotony.

The hall was as warm as the rest of the duplex, the thermostat set to maximum in the hopes I'd actually *feel* the

146

heat. Centuries had passed since I'd felt anything but cold. Now, I wanted to feel more.

Perhaps my turn of mind was due to Tiff and the end of my uncertainty being so close for the first time.

Or maybe I'd just had enough.

It didn't matter, I was caught in limbo, buffeting between relief that my wait was nearly over and caution, because hell, I'd been cocky and convinced once before, and that had left me pants down before the entire coven.

I wouldn't follow that same blinkered path again.

I released the catch then opened the door.

The figure hunched against the cold—more rain, courtesy of the wettest December in thirty-plus years—but without question, I recognized her.

Blonde curls formed ringlets, dripping rain onto her bright red galoshes. She pushed back the hood and looked up. Her eyes were wide and the bluest of opals. Not the lackluster brand of gem, but the kind that made me think of wild oceans and tropical tempests.

She shivered and I grabbed her elbow, pulling her out of the cold.

"Damn, Tiff. You're frozen."

"It wasn't raining when I started out." Her teeth chattered.

"Let's get you out of your clothes and warmed up." I reached for her sopping jacket but she pulled back, halting me with a raise of her hand.

I froze. Her trembling lips were pale, as pale as her skin, but for the blood red slashing her cheeks. I watched as the color slowly spread across her face.

She blinked, then straightened her until now hunched spine. "I'll do it."

25

TIFFANY

rost had all but claimed my brain. Much as Gideon's hall was warm, the cold, hard reality of what I was about to do set like ice in my blood.

I was an idiot, but how could I condemn him to an eternity of hell when there was something I could do to save him? And really, was it that much of a sacrifice? Wouldn't I experience another mind-blowing orgasm along the way?

Another vision.

Maybe that's what this madness was all about. *The vision.* The promise of something more. Maybe *more* was something I wanted after all.

A future filled with the smiles my mother had missed. A future without Richard.

Yesterday, I'd stood up to Richard in a way I never had in the past. I'd felt safe from his fists. Gideon's presence had done that.

"You'll do what?" He stood there, large, proud, with more strength than Richard held in a toenail, let alone a toe.

Yet I didn't feel half the fear I felt when in the company of my ex.

"I'll do it. I'll help make you mortal."

Hope filled his expression, much as he tried to hold it back. From one hopeless hopeful to another, I could spot the need a mile away.

"Are you sure?"

I nodded. Because if I spoke, I wasn't sure what would come out.

"Is it weird for me to say thank you?"

"No more weird than this whole situation." I shivered. Cold, inside and out. "So, what do we do now?"

He reached out, touched my arms, rubbed his hands up and down. "We get you warm."

I followed him into the kitchen, shedding my jacket.

He glanced back. "Your usual?"

I nodded. Confounded. Confused. The more I waited, the more the nerves attacked. There were other, more *active* ways of warming up.

Why was Gideon delaying? The sooner he changed, the better, right? So, why wasn't he pushing to do . . . the thing? Whatever it was that we had to do to save him.

I don't know what I'd imagined when I set out. Ravaging, perhaps. Him jumping my bones, and me being quite open to the fact. The thought heated places that he'd heated so thoroughly, so deliciously, was it only seven nights ago?

He slid a mug across the counter and I wrapped its warmth between my palms. The liquid slipped between my lips, burning a bitter, roasted path down my throat.

"Better?"

"Yeah." One more gulp, then I released the mug. My shaky fingers slipped first one shirt button free, then the next. "How do we do this?"

With a grin, he moved forward and covered my hands. "Slowly." He redid the buttons, and his barely-there touch teased my nipples into taut, hungry buds. My breasts grew heavy, my skin hot and hungry.

His nostrils flared. Could he smell my need?

He stepped away, although the heat in his expression said he'd rather stay. "First, we get to know each other."

"Why? I thought it was just sex."

"No, it's more than sex. It has to mean more. In the words of The Prophesy, *'When love and lust collide, all you hold dear will unfold. Surrender heart, body and soul to bind as one till days of old.'* We'll be bound—heart, body and soul—to each other. We'll share our lives, share a bed. This doesn't end with the ceremony, it begins."

Fuck.

That was a lot of binding and sharing—more than I'd vowed ever to allow. Still, it wasn't as if I believed in love and all that bullshit. I wasn't saving myself for someone else —I didn't want anyone. Didn't need anyone.

So, completing this ceremony and tying myself to Gideon—what did it mean for me?

He formed a barrier to Richard—a very muscular, very mind-melting barrier—offering safety and security I hadn't felt in three years. Truth be told, since before then, even. In addition, there was the added perk of his prowess in the bedroom. And on a bike. That was a big—BIG—plus.

There seemed more arguments for than against. It wasn't as if I couldn't pull the plug if things turned sour.

If I walked away, I had no idea what that meant for Gideon. Then again, if I walked, it'd be his doing, so he'd have to suffer the consequences. Not that he'd ever given me reason to believe he'd turn bad.

Then again, neither had Richard.

Fuck. Why the hell had fate led me to that bastard? My heart smacked against my ribs. He'd screwed me to hell and back, was still screwing me. I'd walked away from his lessons and used the experience as a measure of life's trials, of men, of shit to never allow into my life again. The only power he wielded was the power I gave him.

I had to stop handing him my power on a goddam silver platter.

Maybe that's why he kept coming back. He fed on my fear like a werewolf feeds on the flesh of its victims.

"Hey." Gideon's palm cupped my elbow, a mere touch, a caress almost, warming, calming the gallop of my heart. "I know, it's a lot to take in. Are you still okay with this?"

Was I?

Distance kept my heart intact and my head on track. It was my go-to protection mechanism. And it had worked well the past three years, till Gideon. If he broached that distance, if we got to know each other, what did that mean for distance? For keeping my head and heart out of the equation?

Questions for later. For now, I'd go with the promise of safety and sex. The foundations of my decision.

But there was one thing I needed to clarify first.

"I won't fall in love with you."

His gaze shuttered. "I won't expect you to."

"Good." Why did the twinge in my gut mismatch my

words? I pushed the feeling and every thought that made me question my discontent at his response. He was making it easy. Wasn't that a good thing? "I'll let you know if and when I have a problem."

"I wouldn't expect anything less."

The situation was surreal. We were discussing our upcoming *mating* much the same way we'd discuss a date. Or a dinner menu.

He topped up my drink, then we moved from the kitchen, down a dark, cornice-edged hall and into a living area adorned with rich, red rugs, heavy velvet drapes and a roaring fire. I dropped into a large, voluminous couch and he dropped down beside me. "Tell me about Richard."

"*We* aren't about him."

"Perhaps. But "truth and honor abound" means we need to be open with one another."

I huffed, not wholly as bothered as the huff suggested. "It was so much easier when we were all about sex."

"Oh, we're still about sex. But we're about more, too."

Funny. The *more* didn't chill half as much as it had in the past.

I sighed. "Soon after I graduated from University of Washington, I landed a job with a large pharmaceutical company. Richard was my boss." I hugged my mug to my chest, the warmth seeping through my clothes not strong enough to warm my blood. "Most of my friends were scattered far and wide, so I knew no one local. Richard seemed nice, so when he asked me out, I accepted. Soon, my only friends were his friends, any and all social life revolved around him. He isolated me and I never even saw it. We dated, I fell in love, then I moved in."

Gideon nodded and sipped his drink sans comment. I

was thankful for that. I didn't need any judgements to reinforce what a trusting fool I'd been back then.

"A week later, I arrived home late from a hair appointment. The first blow struck me on the side of the head and took me totally by surprise." I swallowed, the bitter taste of blood from that first strike still fresh on my tongue. "My head spun so fast, I didn't have the wherewithal to react. So, he punched me, this time in the stomach. He spat words at me. *Whore. Cheat. Liar.* Then he hit me again, then three times more, until I curled up on the floor at his feet, a quivering, quaking, blubbering mess. Then he dropped to his knees, kissed my bruised face and swore he'd never do it again." I inhaled, my lungs so constricted my vision turned to stars. "That was the first time I believed his lies."

The cool touch of Gideon's hand warmed me. I didn't need anyone, but it was nice to have someone all the same.

"How long did you stay?"

"It took me a year to realize that no matter how much he apologized and no matter how much I trusted, the Richard I knew in the beginning was never coming back."

"Probably because he never existed."

"I know that now. It just took me twelve months of stupidity to find out."

"Not stupidity. Strength. It takes an amazing person to put up with that kind of crap. And an amazing person to realize she deserves more." He squeezed my hand, and it was like he squeezed my heart. "Everyone deserves to trust without fear."

Emotion welled in my throat, making it difficult to breathe, but I managed two words all the same. "Thank you."

"What for?"

I swallowed. "For not asking why I stayed so long. For not telling me I should have left sooner."

He shrugged, acting as if his blameless response were the norm. "Why would I judge? I wasn't there."

"That's never stopped people in the past."

"I'm not 'people.'"

The more time I spent with Gideon, the more I had to agree. "No, you're definitely not 'people.'" Only dregs remained in my mug. I'd stayed way longer than I'd planned. "I should go."

"Stay."

My heartbeat stuttered. "For the ceremony?"

"No. For us."

"You mean sex."

"No. Just to be together and for whatever follows."

I had no idea what that meant, but something in me softened at the suggestion. I didn't want to be alone, not tonight.

Realization drifted in on the wings of hope. Because after the ceremony, I never had to be alone again.

We'd had sex, twice. Hot, heady, mountain-moving sex that had rocked not only my body, but every foundation that gave me strength.

If before it had moved mountains, this shattered me to the core.

Wrapped in one of Gideon's shirts, I crawled into his bed and snuggled into his arms. My heart struck up a staccato beat, but my breathing escaped long and slow. Fresh, woodsy aromas filled my nostrils, earth and pine with a dash of citrus, and undertones of something deeper, something intrinsically male and undeniably Gideon.

I hadn't actually slept with a man for three years. I'd fucked and left, but never stayed. Now I was staying without the preamble, and my brain had no idea what to do with that. I lay on my side, my head resting on his shoulder, my ear so close to his mouth I could feel every cool breath as it left his lips.

Much as he'd urged me to spoon I'd refused. I didn't turn my back to any man in bed. Some habits were harder to surrender.

His hand twisted lazily in my hair. "Okay?"

Was I? Did I even know what okay entailed? I was comfortable. Calm. Drowsily horny, heat seeping through my body in a languorous, lethargic swirl. If that constituted okay, then I guess I had my answer. "Yes."

"Good."

Light crept in through the partially open door, allowing me to watch the flutter of his lashes as his eyes closed. His breathing deepened. The hand playing with my hair slackened, but not once did it let me go.

I watched the rise and fall of his chest. The play of shadows on his bedroom wall. Leaving the hall light on had been Gideon's idea, motivated by his concern that I'd wake and feel disoriented. I knew he'd meant scared, and his concession had sparked a play of moisture to blur my vision.

I stroked his chest, the skin cold, devoid of blood's warmth and the throb of a beating heart. Impossible to equate this Gideon with the notion of a vampire. If I hadn't seen the change in his eyes, the baring of his fangs . . . I was sleeping with a vampire, promising a commitment that went deeper than any wedding ceremony I'd sworn to avoid.

Once upon a time, I'd have questioned the sense that saw me so willing to fall asleep in a man's arms. Now I wondered if it was sense that had convinced me to stay.

26

GIDEON

Three hundred years, and I'd never slept as soundly as I did with Tiff wrapped in my arms.

I could have said I'd lain there for hours, listening to her breathing, marveling in the wonder of finally finding her. In reality, she'd rested her head in the crook of my arm, and within seconds I'd dozed off, spicy vanilla filling my nostrils, a feeling of peace filling my chest.

My lifetime of searching was finally over.

That didn't stop me from waking with a raging hard-on and an insatiable need to sink balls-deep into her body. It's possible this was sparked by the slide of her hand up and down my cock, although I imagine just her close proximity and wearing nothing but my shirt would have done the trick.

Her gaze glittered with carnal promise and not once did her hand stop its erotic glide. "You're up nice and early." She squeezed and my eyes all but rolled back in my head.

"Fffuck." The word escaped in an oxygen-starved hiss.

"My thoughts exactly." She dipped her head, her lips curving into a sassy, cock-tugging smile. "And if we can't perform the actual act, I'm sure there are other activities we can enjoy equally."

Fuck me if she didn't slither down my body and draw my cock into her sweet, sultry mouth. I near bucked clear from the bed. My fangs descended as her lips closed tight over my shaft, working tip to balls, milking me towards bursting. Arousal—hers, mine—filled my nostrils, the tang of her thrumming blood taunting my taste buds. Her tongue did this swirly, skating thing up and down my length as she sucked and fucked me until I came deep in her throat.

She drank and swallowed every last drop, then licked her lips as if feasting on some decadent dessert.

When I found Tiff, I'd not only found salvation, I'd found heaven as well.

I dragged my mind back to the moment and retracted my fangs. She might know what I was, but she didn't need the reality shoved in her face. And I didn't need her rejection of my other self again. Not now.

She slithered up my body, a cat got the cream grin on her face. "That's breakfast done."

I brushed the hair back from her brow. "You're wicked, woman."

"I was hungry, I ate. What's so wicked about that?"

"No complaints here. Any time you're hungry, just say the word. I'll be happy to oblige." I lifted a knee, rolling her onto her back, wedging her body tight between my thighs. "I've just realized, I'm a little peckish myself."

I scrunched up her shirt, then eased it off, baring her breasts, feasting first on one, then the other. She moaned, squeezing the plump, rounded flesh, peaking her nipples, so tight, so firm against my tongue.

Sweet, heady musk wafted up from between her thighs,

and I wanted its taste on my tongue more than my next breath. Our mating would make this a reality. Its imminence filled my chest. But for now . . .

She parted her legs as I edged downwards. Her fingers cut through my hair, pushing my face deeper into her sweet, succulent flesh. I licked, ass to clit, and she mewled. I swirled my tongue round that tight knot of nerves and she shuddered. Then I slid my tongue into her pussy before sucking and swirling some more, and she screamed. I pressed one finger inside, then two, and her hips bucked up to meet me. I added another finger, stretching her, separating her labia, opening her further to the ministrations of my tongue.

Her breath quickened, her racing heartbeat calling to my baser instincts.

I pumped and sucked and swirled, feeding on her frenzy, on her cries to fuck and suck and push her over the edge of sanity. Her body stretched, then stiffened, her pussy tumbling into contractions that pulled my fingers harder and deeper into her flesh.

I didn't stop until her fumbling hands scrabbled at my hair, urging me up.

Good sex was great, but there was nothing as satisfying as a woman coming against your tongue. The scent, the tang, the texture far surpassed anything I'd encountered over my three-hundred plus years of life.

I crawled back up her body and covered her parted lips with mine. She kissed me, no holding back, the scent of my cum melding with the lingering scent of hers. I pulled back, gasping, and rolled off, collapsing semi-conscious beside her. "You taste better than any breakfast I've experienced."

She turned her head and grinned, her chest still rapidly

rising and falling, her cheeks dusted in red, her hair tousled and awry about her face. "That's one helluva wake up call."

"I aim to please."

"That, you do."

I turned onto my side, resting my head on one hand, running the fingers of the other across her warm, live skin. "How are you feeling this morning?"

"After that orgasm, pretty fucking awesome."

I chuckled. "Good to hear. But that's not quite what I meant." I circled her nipple with my fingertips, watching it pucker and harden, my cock mimicking its action. One benefit of possessing superhuman strength—it wasn't solely isolated to muscles above the waist. It wouldn't take long for me to harden and want her again.

My breath hitched. Tiff was all about the sexual. Would my mortal self be as able as my vampire to satisfy her? I hadn't considered what other changes would materialize with mortality. When I traded in my vampire fangs and appetite, would I lose other benefits I'd long since taken for granted?

Food for thought if I was to hold onto Tiff and keep her happy past our mating.

I walked my fingers over her ribs, down and around her belly button, reveling in her hitched breath and the tightening of muscles beneath my touch. "I know this whole 'commit your life and save a vampire' situation was pretty much thrust upon you. I just want to know that you're okay with it all."

Her body stiffened. "I think so." She turned, dislodging my hand to mirror my position. "I'm still processing the implications, but with mornings like this, I think I'm more than okay."

160

It was her protection mechanism—using sex as a diversion. Whether it be in conversation or in the act itself.

I had no clue how to sway her need to safeguard herself with me. The Prophesy spoke of "love and essence." Whether the word love spoke to the act or the emotion, I hadn't a clue. I sensed Tiff had moved from animosity to like, but was that enough to fulfil the requirements of our mating ritual?

Did she wonder at my reticence to bond? I could continue to let her believe I was allowing her the time she needed to adjust. In reality, my motives were less than altruistic. I delayed in the hope that her like would soon slide into love.

There were no issues on my side. I'd loved her since discovering the idea of her. And the reality of my soulmate far surpassed my imagination. Tiff was sexy and funny and saucy and sweet. She stirred my senses as well as my mind.

The idea of mating and sharing my life with anyone else was unimaginable.

I walked my fingers across the pillow, allowing the tips to brush the mark on her neck that made her mine. "Breakfast in bed has always been a favorite activity of mine." I shot her a grin and took a leap of faith. "What do you have going on at work today?"

Her expression clouded. It had to be the memory of her douche ex and his gleeful announcement. Damn the bastard for slipping his smarmy existence into our bed.

I scraped my knuckles up over Tiff's hips and down over her waist to distract her from her less than savory thoughts. "Let's do something special today. Wanna be naughty and play hooky?"

In less than thirty seconds her hesitation turned to

decision. "What do you have in mind?" She reached across, swirling her fingertips over my chest, grazing her nails back and forth over my nipple until I felt every scrape deep down in my balls.

She was distracting again, and fuck me, it was working.

I dragged my thoughts back to our conversation. "Tell me something you've always wanted to do but haven't had the chance."

"I'm glad you asked." Her fingers grazed downwards, circling my stomach, then lower still to my already straining cock. "I have this fantasy. It involves chocolate caramel sauce, lots of skin, and lots and lots of licking." She licked her palm, then returned it to my cock, wrapping her fingers round tight, squeezing until I was close to bursting.

My voice lodged halfway down my throat as her hand began to pump, but I managed a few strained words. "I was thinking activities outside the bedroom."

"Honey, you can lick me anywhere you like."

She was so fucking hot. And tempting. And freaking insatiable.

Her blood pumped double time through her veins, the pulse at her neck beckoning for me to taste.

Not yet.

It was too soon.

If she could like me, then there was the possibility she could love me. I had to believe it, not only for The Prophesy, but for me. Because living my one and only mortal life in love with a woman who didn't love me back would be worse than living an eternity still searching.

27

TIFFANY

or three years I'd lived in a city dubbed the Sportsman's Paradise, less than half an hour from Lake Pontchartrain, yet I'd never ventured onto the water.

Gideon changed that.

I clung to his leather-clad body, reveling in the glorious play of muscles beneath my palms as he maneuvered his motorcycle towards the lake. We crossed the causeway—another first. He parked, dragged a picnic basket from the bike's saddle bag, then led me towards the marina and a pretty white houseboat with *The Merry Molly* inscribed on the side. "What do you think?"

"Your mother?"

He nodded.

"Molly's Irish, isn't it?"

Again he nodded, staring up at the pale blue lattice just below the roofline. "Her family fled Ulster in the early 1700s in search of a better life. She loved the water and wanted to settle in Maryland, but she ended up in Pennsylvania instead.

Lucky for me, because that's where she met and married Dad. They built a life there, worked, had kids, died. They're buried there too, in a double grave." He dropped his gaze. "She never did get to the water. I guess this is my way of giving her in death what she never achieved in life."

Every word was like fluffy pink cotton candy, filling and feeding my heart. "That's beautiful, Gideon. If she were here, I'm sure she'd be mega-proud of her son."

He swallowed. "I like to think so." He grabbed my hand. "Come. Let me show you around *The Merry Molly*."

We stepped onto the wraparound veranda, immediately experiencing the roll of the water beneath. My body swayed and I fell against him. He grinned, dropping the basket, wrapping his arm around my waist, pulling me hard against his solid, powerful frame. "Got your sea legs?"

His breath fanned my cheek, his hand dipping lower to cup my ass.

Fuck.

Was it bad I wanted to straddle him like a thoroughbred racehorse and ride his cock till his knees buckled and my body liquefied into a lusty puddle at his feet? Gideon had become my new favorite obsession, and I doubted I'd ever get tired. Sammy had well and truly retired to the back of my underwear drawer. I doubted he'd ever see the light of day again.

I lifted a leg—thankful for my sensible slacks and top combo—wrapping it around his thighs, pressing hard against his erection.

Holy fuck. He was big and firm and oh, so thick. And he wielded his cock like a warrior wields his sword.

I rubbed my pant-covered pussy up his length. Wet heat flooded the swollen folds, ready for him to fill me and make me whole. I kissed his neck, then his ear, laving and sucking him towards submission. "Fuck me, Gideon."

He groaned, dropping his forehead to mine, his breathing just as ragged, his body just as ready. "What about my surprise?"

"I can feel it, all nine inches."

His laughter rumbled through my flesh and I wanted to bottle it and keep it to remind me how good life could be.

Slowly, reluctantly, he dropped me down. "You have no idea how hard this is."

I reached between us and cupped him through his cargos. "I have some idea."

"Hold onto that thought." His gaze turned gold as he peeled my hand from his cock. "Today is about firsts. Believe me, when it's time, you'll be glad we didn't do this now." He dropped a kiss to the tip of my nose. "It'll be great, I promise."

I wasn't so sure that was true, but I had to trust him.

My heart flip-flopped in my chest.

Trust.

Since when did I link that word with any man?

Yet, here I was, ready to trust Gideon. The circumstances weren't earth-shattering or world-changing. This was about his word. But since his whole vampire-reveal, he'd given me no reason to question. And if we were bound by fate until death do we part, shouldn't I at least give him the benefit of the doubt?

Now seemed as good a time as any. "Fine. But just know, I'm so, so wet. All I can think about right now is your cock sliding into my pussy, deep and hard and over and over until I shake and shudder and scream out your name."

His body trembled and I couldn't help but smile. He was

as insatiable as I. We wanted with the same ferocity, and we fucked with the same fire.

It wasn't difficult to believe the universe deemed us a pair.

Something clicked when I was with Gideon. We made sense, we made sparks and a multitude of orgasms, which were endless and always, *always* better than the last.

He pulled back. "I haven't got a cold shower but I have the next best thing." He grinned as he led me into a large, open living space. He held up a wetsuit.

"We're going swimming?"

"Nope. Water skiing."

"And this is better than sex?"

"It's the lead-up to sex. I won't let you down."

He hadn't so far in that department. No reason to believe he'd do it now. "I'm holding you to that."

His glorious lips twitched. "I wouldn't have it any other way."

I took the suit, not at all sure this day was going the way I'd planned. When he'd suggested we play hooky, I'd imagined sex, instead he was taking me skiing.

Ever tried to slip into a wetsuit when you're horny as all hell? It's about as difficult as squeezing a banana back into its unbroken skin. Gideon's hands smoothed the rubber up and over my body—totally unhelpful. As was the glint in his eyes which said he was enjoying my discomfort way too much.

Then again, the wrap of wetsuit rubber around his groin said he was just as uncomfortable.

Next came the lessons.

First we practiced on the houseboat. I slipped into the skis, gripped an imaginary handle, squatted and braced.

When he was convinced I'd mastered the technique, he unhooked a large cuddy cabin from behind *The Merry Molly* and we made for the middle of the lake.

It hadn't seemed too hard back on solid—slightly swaying—ground.

Of course, that was before water resistance forced my legs to slide in opposite directions, planting my face flat in the path of the water spray.

Not. Much. Fun. If this was Gideon's surprise, I was so not impressed.

It took thirteen tries before I skied for an entire six seconds without toppling head over ass. The triumph didn't sway my relief when he announced it was time for lunch.

We moored just inside the mouth of Tchefuncte River, a peaceful, private setting that made me feel as if we were the last two people remaining in the world.

"Enjoy it?"

My thighs still ached and my knees still quivered. "*Enjoy* might be a stretch."

He quirked a brow, placing container after container of food onto a rug on the floor of the cabin. First came mini muffulettas, each round sesame bread stuffed with olive salad and thick layers of cheeses and meats. "I thought you liked skiing."

"Not without snow and a slope."

He unpacked a small tray of beignets—their light, flaky pastry enticingly dusted with powdered sugar. Last came a selection of fresh fruits and nuts, some sodas and mineral water. "But you can water ski minus the cold."

"Which just goes to show you can't have everything."

"Not quite true."

The basket was empty but for one final container. He brandished it with a grin.

My heartbeat turned staccato, my body melting with mere thoughts of what Gideon had planned. "Caramel sauce?"

He waggled his brows. "With swirls of chocolate."

"For me?"

"For both of us."

"Would you be terribly upset if we skipped lunch and went straight to dessert?"

He flipped the lid and rich, decadent caramel filled my nostrils. "I thought you'd never ask."

A little corner of my heart melted.

It wasn't the drizzle of sauce over my skin. Or the play of Gideon's tongue teasing my flesh towards ecstasy. It wasn't the slow burn as he stoked the fire that roared through my blood as I climaxed not once, but thrice. It wasn't even the reverence he bestowed while worshipping every quivering inch of my body.

No. It was none of that.

It was Gideon planning an entire day with the sole purpose of pleasing me.

The skiing—much as it involved water instead of snow —the picnic, the *sauce*. Gideon had heard—*he'd listened*— he'd taken note, and he'd acted. When had anyone gone to that much trouble, *for me?*

The ski boat—named *The Dan,* after his father—rolled and bucked with the waves. He pushed the food aside and lay me out on the rug like a feast he fully intended to ravage. I quivered at the thought. *Damn, I hope so.*

My body heated beneath his gaze, the sweep of a cool breeze tormenting my skin, plumping my breasts and peaking my nipples into tight, hungry buds.

Gideon kneeled beside me, his gaze a glittering gold. I now recognized the tight set of his jaw showed how much he fought the release of his vampire self.

My heart warmed with his care, even while part of me wanted his vampire to emerge, wanted his fangs to sink deep into my flesh, awakening the visions that had haunted and captivated me since that erotic, unforgettable night.

"The trick to creating the perfect dessert is all about design." Gideon dipped his finger into the container, then brought the dripping sauce to his lips. My mouth watered.

He dipped again, this time rubbing the sauce along my lips until I opened my mouth and sucked away every last drop.

My gaze dropped to his cock, just inches from my face, the thick, hard tip tenting the fabric of his black board shorts. If I leaned over, I could open my mouth and take him inside, savoring the sweet and sour of his essence across my tongue.

"Placement is the key." His hand hovered above me and thick, cool liquid drizzled from his fingertip. My breath hitched, my body thrummed. My gaze riveted to that finger, that dripping sauce, my body waiting, craving, anticipating each and every drop.

I trembled.

Sauce dripped onto my skin, oozing out over my breasts. They swelled, heavy, achy, my already tight nipples constricting towards pain. Another scoop, and the cool trickle rolled over my belly, seeping down towards the V between my thighs. I parted my legs, tilting my hips, exposing my throbbing flesh to the cool breeze and a third scoop of gooey gloriousness. My pussy clenched. Empty. Grasping. Needy.

I moaned.

The spill and slide of the sauce was incredible, but I wanted—*needed*—more.

"Gideon."

His gaze latched to mine. "Command me."

Fuck.

He scooped up one final dollop and dropped it between my parted lips. It drizzled over my chin, down my neck, joining the sauce still taunting my breasts.

I swallowed, then pushed up, sliding my hand behind his head, pulling him down to meet me. His kiss was one of submission, yet he possessed me as sure as if he'd cast me with some spell. He drank from my mouth, our lips taking, our tongues dancing, his taste as decadent as the chocolate caramel he'd used to slake my hunger.

He pulled back. "Tell me what you want."

My heart smacked against my ribs. His gaze glinted iridescent, pulling me under whatever voodoo magic he wove, stealing my breath and every thought bar one. *"Eat me."*

Without a word he dipped his mouth to my breast and sucked.

Holy fuck.

The wet of the sauce and the pull of his mouth dragged at my pussy, liquefying every inch of my body. Every lick, every suck, every pull dragged me deeper into mindlessness, over the edge of reason to a place from which I could never return.

His tongue circled my belly button, sucking and fucking it until the flesh between my thighs cried out with jealousy. My pussy pulsed, avaricious, needy.

I slipped my hand across my thigh only to have it purposefully removed.

"Tell me what you want."

My dry throat crackled, but I managed three words. "*Eat my pussy.*"

With a grin, he dropped his head and followed my bidding. He nipped and swirled, nibbled and tugged, his fingers stroking spots A through to G until I came in a thunderous rush, my body arched, cries of pleasure bursting through my lips.

Two times more, he stoked, he stroked and brought me to pleasure. Each time more thunderous, more earthshattering than the last. As my body arched one final time, his arm slid up and around my waist, easing my quivering frame down onto the rug.

I collapsed. Shattered. Sticky. Thoroughly satisfied. "Holy fuck."

"I take it you appreciated my surprise?"

I could hear the smile in his voice and it flip-flopped my heart, even as my body continued to float on the post-climactic swirl of fluffy, white clouds. On a long exhale, I murmured my response. "Any time you feel compelled to surprise me again, go ahead. I am now officially, totally, irrevocably in love with surprises."

"Good to know." Gideon's deep rumble floated through a haze bordering on wakefulness.

The boat's dip and roll lulled me into lethargy.

My eyelids fluttered, my breath rolling out from somewhere deep in my chest. A wet cloth swept in small, circular strokes over my skin. My head lifted, then slowly lowered onto something soft and springy, and velvety warmth wrapped deliciously around my body.

Light receded into dark, and I tumbled into slumber, my last thoughts filled with the man who'd given me hopes for a future beyond my wildest imagination.

28

GIDEON

*T*he *Dan's* engine rumbled beneath my feet.

If I'd had a live, beating heart, it would have been hammering double time. As it was, my body thrummed with what could have been mistaken for life.

Love.

She'd said the word. Not quite in the way I'd hoped, but she'd still said it. She *loved* what I'd done. Could I stretch that to mean she loved *me* doing what I'd done? That maybe she'd come to love me in time, too?

I held onto that hope.

I steered the hull into the marina, slowing to allow old Hal passage in his battered black and blue catamaran. He blared the horn and waved as he passed.

The body beneath the blanket stirred. Indigo perfect eyes fluttered open, her pale pink lips slipping easily into a smile. "Hey."

"Hey."

She yawned and stretched. "I can't believe I fell asleep. How long was I out?" Her fingertips reached high over her head, her toe tips extending just shy of the stern. The blanket slipped allowing the tips of her nipples to play peek-a-boo with my libido.

I dragged my attention back to the marina and to maneuvering *The Dan* safely into its moorings behind *The Molly*. "Not long. About an hour."

"You wore me out." She pushed up onto her elbows and the blanket fell away.

My cock stirred. "Is that a complaint?"

"Absolutely not!"

I cut the engine, wrapped the blanket round her body and pulled her up into my arms. I kissed the tip of her nose and resisted moving my kisses to her neck and down over her delectable breasts. "We should get some clothes on you and head back. I want to show you something on the way."

She dressed and I helped. Or maybe I hindered. The process spanned over an hour and a couple of shared orgasms, instead of a few minutes. When we finally mounted my bike, luminous pink-purple rays stretched out across the darkening sky.

We left the causeway and turned onto Route 10.

In less than half an hour we rode past the cast iron archway of the cemetery towards an entrance only few knew existed.

I grabbed the picnic basket in one hand and Tiff's hand in the other, leading her through the gap in the fence. It took only five minutes of weaving amidst rows of crumbling stone and tombs the size of beach boxes, the sweet tang of swamp ferns and wild violets rising up to greet us. Then we came to the spot.

My spot.

For years I'd visited alone, watching the number of

graves grow, contemplating my life, the shit I'd been handed, a wayward gene that had ripped me from my world. It seemed fitting that the first person to share my sanctuary was the one who could save me from the horrors I sought to escape.

"What is this place?"

I dropped her hand to spread a new, non-caramel covered rug out over the grass verge within the heritage wrought iron fencing. The tomb rose up before us, lit by a dull green light from its base, the words *'Amor in vita et morte'* carved above the large, weather-worn headstone.

Love in life and death. Fitting in so many ways.

I began unpacking the remnants of our uneaten lunch. "The last resting place of the Williams family."

"You knew them?"

"Only in death."

She dropped onto the rug wearing an *are you nuts* expression. "What does that mean?"

I passed her a muffuletta, taking one for myself, only to drop it back into the container. The thought of food made my normally robust stomach churn. "When I first discovered what I was, I ran from my life. I thought if I ran hard enough, fast enough, I could outrun reality, find some sense of peace and acceptance somewhere in the world. Surely it existed?" I glanced down at the white of my knuckles and forced my hand to unclench. "It took me over a century before I realized I couldn't run from my fate. I returned to the US, and soon after I stumbled on the cemetery. I was still angry at the world, at fate, at the circumstances that had ended my life. Then I stumbled on this plot."

Tiff devoured her sandwich without once shifting her gaze from me. She licked her lips and grabbed a beignet, digging in with unrestrained relish. Not surprising. She hadn't eaten since breakfast. The last time I'd finished a meal with even a smidge of her satisfaction was too long in the past to recall how it felt. That I might experience the feeling once again—and soon—made my head spin.

My gaze roamed, scanning the crumbling remains of nearby tombs, weeds and flowers alike, scrabbling for life amongst the paved pathways and centuries-worn cement. Time and the elements had been less than kind.

I grabbed a mineral water and chugged back the greater portion. "Back then there were fewer graves and even fewer visitors. The cemetery wasn't the cash cow it is now." I stared at the half empty bottle, watching the bubbles rise, scrabbling to escape their confinement. "The tomb was new, less than a week old. When I read the inscription, their tragedy spoke to mine. But where my family had been torn apart, they'd remained together, in both life and death, sharing their fate. The youngest, little Johnny, was six weeks old when the yellow fever took him. He'd barely lived before he died."

"How sad."

I nodded, a familiar weight slumping heavily in my chest. "I often sit here and pretend I'm a regular person, living a regular life, visiting my family's grave. Not a vampire whose parents died centuries ago."

It felt good to finally share a part of my existence I'd fearfully hidden from the world for so long.

Her hand covered mine with a warmth no fire could replicate. "I can't imagine what that must be like. Never ageing. Outliving the people you love."

I wrapped my fingers tightly around hers. "After a while, it was easier to shut off from the world rather than let others in. I'd only lose them in the end. It wasn't as if I could explain why I didn't wrinkle and gray over the years at the same rate they did."

Her grip on my hand tightened. "Soon that part of your life will be over."

"I've waited so long. Now the moment's almost here, I can't imagine what life will be like."

"Don't the visions tell you?"

I shook my head. "I've never had visions."

"Never? Not even when you bit me and voodooed a vision into my brain?"

I grinned. "I didn't 'voodoo' anything, and I definitely never had any visions." She'd previously mentioned visions, but I'd never taken much notice before now. Partners pre-Tiff had never mentioned them. Then again, partners pre-Tiff weren't part of The Prophesy and my soon-to-be mortal future. "What did you see?"

She scrunched her nose. It looked so goddam cute that I leaned over and kissed it.

She pulled back. "What was that for?"

"Nothing more than I wanted to kiss you."

She leaned over and kissed me right back, this time on the lips.

"What was that for?"

"Ditto."

"Ditto?"

"Yeah." She grinned.

I grinned back. If mating meant trading countless immortal lifetimes for just one lifetime of this, I was in.

But I'd born the weight of The Change for so long, how would it feel to live without the fear of when and where? To feel free.

I brushed my thumb back and forth across the knuckles of the woman responsible for lifting that weight. "What did you see?"

"Nothing . . . *concrete*. More *impressions*, really. Emotions, even. The vision seemed so real at the time, but if I try and put what I saw into words, it makes little sense."

"I'd really like to know."

Again she scrunched her nose. "It was like . . . rainbows. An entire row of them. All bright but broken and dark in places. Yet the end of each one shone with light that felt like happiness. Fulfillment. A life I'd wanted as a child but stopped believing in long since I'd become an adult."

"What kind of life?"

She froze and snaked her hand free, snagging a beignet. Did that whole bubble-blowing, mouth opening and closing fish thing, which said she didn't know whether to speak or remain silent.

I grabbed a handful of pecans to avoid saying something stupid and swaying her either way. Sharing had to be her decision.

She inhaled. Long. Slow. Then met my gaze. "A home. A family. Someone who loves me. Kids who depend on me." Her hands clenched so tight in her lap, crumbling the pastry, turning her knuckles waxen and white. "All of us living a life, safe and secure, never knowing the wrong end of a fist or words meant to cut you to a mere fragment of your original self."

29

TIFFANY

I'd said too much.

I heard it in the awkward silence following my outburst. I saw it in Gideon's expression. I felt it as the old hurts reared up and stabbed at my already aching heart.

Would I ever leave that part of my life behind?

The sharp lines in Gideon's expression softened. "This is about more than just Richard, isn't it?"

I shivered, cold in my blood far out-chilling the absence of the sun's rays. "I'd rather not talk about it."

"I get that." He raised a palm to stall me from further comment. "I won't push you to share."

I hadn't realized my hand was so tightly clenched until it loosened, releasing pastry crumbs and powdered sugar all over my lap. The last thing I'd expected was acceptance.

I nodded, my "thank you" caught somewhere in the back of my throat.

"Saying that, after disclosing certain facts about myself to a certain person . . ." His grin whittled away at some of the chill. "I've learned that sharing has the potential to strip pain of its powers. If whatever occurred in the past is still influencing your present, it may help to find someone you trust and talk about it." He shot me a half-smile when I didn't react. "It doesn't have to be me."

I nodded and tried to look like I was considering his suggestion. What else could I do? Family skeletons belonged six-feet under, dead and buried, left to rot in the ground, not in my goddam head. And not in my new goddam life.

A hand gently unfurled my fist. "Come here." Gideon edged over and beckoned me to do the same. I shuffled around and backwards, reclining between his legs, his hard, sculpted stomach contracting against my spine, his cock resting deliciously between my butt cheeks. He wrapped me in his arms and I hugged them to my chest.

His cool breath ruffled my hair.

Birdsong floated on the wings of the breeze. Leaves rustled, the wind sighed and my heart thudded loudly in my chest.

Stars sprinkled the sky above.

Time rolled by. Seconds. Minutes. Each breath, each heartbeat marking passing moments that held little or no meaning while I basked in Gideon's arms.

Tours had long since finished in the other, less private sections of the cemetery. But for some animal rustling through the undergrowth, perhaps a raccoon or mole, we were completely and utterly alone.

Safe.

I sighed, comfortable. Comforted. If only I could bottle up the entire day and keep it secure, somewhere Richard and the other bruises of my world couldn't reach.

Winter's chill finally cut through the warmth from my

less than adequate clothes and I shivered. He dropped a kiss to my head. "We should go."

Much as I wanted to stay here, away from the rest of the world, in his arms forever, the cold won the battle.

I nodded and stood, pulling him up.

We packed up the picnic, then headed for home. His home. Was it soon-to-be ours? We hadn't spoken of semantics and I wasn't sure it mattered where we lived, only that we would live together. That the peace and openness we'd shared over the course of the day would continue. And maybe Gideon's show of honesty would go some ways to healing a heart still smarting from the lies of the past.

The day had been long, and the night ahead didn't seem long enough.

The sex was unrushed, the aftermath unchecked. We collapsed in each other's arms, and when he turned me, wrapping his arms around me from behind, plastering his body to the back of mine, I ignored the skittery beat of my heart and snuggled in.

As my body slowly returned to earth, reality began to set in. Our day of hooky was nearly at an end.

Tomorrow we'd return to work. So much had changed since I'd last entered the pristine buildings of Hagen Pharmaceuticals.

Richard, for one. I'd uploaded my resume on more than one job search site, and already sent out a couple of tentative enquiries. I'd heard nothing back, but it was still early days.

"I've been thinking."

My lips curved. "An exceedingly dangerous occupation."

He tweaked my nipple.

"Ouch!"

"Behave."

"Or what?"

His hand slid south. "Or not. I happen to enjoy it when you don't behave." He smiled into my neck, stopping just shy of my tummy. "However, I wanted to say . . . I've been thinking about your position at Hagen."

Serenity spilled from my body as if it were river waters tumbling over a fall.

"Would you consider staying on and applying for Mannie's position?"

"No." The word escaped without thought.

"Wow, that was fast."

"I don't need time to think. Richard is toxic, and I've suffered enough toxicity in my life to fill a whole damn dumpsite. Anywhere he is, I don't want to be."

"I get that." He brushed across my belly button in cyclic, barely-there strokes. "Have you considered that the reason Richard still has power over you is because you feed it? Maybe if you stop running and face your fears, you'll cut short not only his chase, but also whatever sick pleasure he derives from seeing you scared. You'll win and he'll lose, and eventually he'll skulk off to whatever hole he crawled out from to lick his wounds."

The idea wasn't new. It wasn't as if I hadn't already realized that I handed Richard opportunity to strike me down every time I showed him my fear. Of course, knowing was one thing. Having the strength to do something about it was entirely different.

"Think about it. If you continue not to face him, you'll spend the rest of your life running." His palm stroked my tummy in slow, circular caresses. "And don't forget, this time will be different, because I'm here for you."

Warm and fuzzy weren't emotions I'd ever indulged, until now. Gideon's presence shouldn't have factored—I'd learned the hard way to rely on no one outside of myself.

But he made it all sound so simple, so easy. And dammit, he was right. The more I ran, the more pleasure Richard derived from intimidating me. His sneering face rose up in my mind. My heart raced, but with less vigor than before. Even the *stupid bitch* spilling from his lips rang with less angst.

Perhaps I could do this.

I'd have been lying if I said working with Gideon, as well as playing with Gideon, didn't sway me. Amazing what great sex and even greater company did for the soul.

I didn't need to make a decision now, but what I could do is make a decision to think on it. It was a start, and one step in a direction I'd never imagined taking before now.

He stroked my waist, my hip, my thigh. "So, what do you say?"

"You want to work with me?"

He paused. "Very much so."

"You won't get bored?"

"Why would I?"

Because every other man I've allowed past first date status has done exactly that.

I had to slap that thought, hard. Gideon wasn't Richard. He'd proven time and time again he outstripped him in every way imaginable.

That included the slow, seductive sweep of his palm back over my hip.

I allowed the sensation to lull me into lethargy, the

cocoon of Gideon's body at my back, his hand doing delicious things to my front.

His mouth stroked sensation over the curve of my shoulder. "Tiff? Will you give it a try?"

I closed my eyes and imagined another life. The life of my vision.

My heart tugged and my mind had no choice but to follow. "Yes."

"*W*hat's this?"

I lowered my book to watch Gideon stride into the bedroom, skin still slicked from his shower, a blue towel slung low on his hips. *Hot fucking hell*. He was gorgeous. My mouth watered automatically. And that wasn't the wettest place on my body.

I dropped my gaze from the wicked glint in his eye to Sammy, wrapped firmly in his very large, very skillful hand. I'd moved him from my underwear drawer to the bathroom cabinet, assuming he'd be safer. I'd been wrong.

"Not what. Who." I crossed my legs—bare but for Gideon's tee resting mid-thigh—and leaned further back against the headboard, trading wicked glint for wicked glint as I rolled my hand through the air. "Gideon, Sammy. Sammy, Gideon."

"It has a name?" He quirked a brow.

I quirked one back. "Of course. Don't all boyfriends?"

"You're kidding."

"Absolutely not. I never kid about sex."

He stared at my old flame—the large, thick shaft, the wide, swollen head, the rabbit-eared stimulator—then flicked the switch. Motorized beads rolled up and down the aqua blue length while the stimulators pulsed and shuddered.

Heat swamped my core, not from the familiar whirr of the motor, or the memory of thick, vibrating silicone sliding into my quivering flesh. Sammy had long been relegated to the shelf, and not once had he been missed.

It was this big, beautiful man, holding my silicone pleasure machine in his hand, making me hotter than an Arizona heatwave.

His nostrils flared in a way that said he'd caught the scent of my arousal, and the slow curve of his lips said he liked it. "Should I be jealous?"

"Only if you doubt your prowess."

He moved closer, the throbbing, rotating shaft still clutched in his hand. "I think my prowess is perfectly intact, considering your screams this morning—was it four times?"

Five, actually. But who's counting?

He glanced from Sammy to me, a teasing tilt to his lips. "Did you love him?"

I shrugged. "He was reliable, dependable and always willing. I wasn't after anything more."

"So, lust then?" He twirled him in his hands, then held him out for me to take. "Show me."

Holy fuckoly.

"You want to watch?"

"I can't think of anything hotter."

My gaze slid down from his hand to the tent in his towel. I grabbed Sammy and edged the hem of my tee upwards. "Lose the towel."

With one flick, it dropped to the floor.

He was glorious. A god. Making me want to drop to my knees and worship every amazing inch.

I knew his texture. His taste. I licked my lips, splayed my legs and eased Sammy between my thighs. Gideon's gaze turned golden.

"Closer."

Two steps and his cock was within reach, fresh from the shower, radiating pine, fresh grass and potent male arousal.

I was so fucking wet. So fucking ready. With slow, steady pressure, I eased Sammy inside, watching the twitch of Gideon's cock, the seep of precum escaping his tip.

"Closer."

One more step and he towered over me. I pushed Sammy deep, his stimulators massaging my clit as I flicked my tongue at Gideon's cock, swirled his head, sucked the tip.

He growled.

I panted, releasing Sammy, then pressing him deep again. In, out, in perfect rhythm with my play on Gideon's cock. One hand still moving Sammy, I reached up with the other and stroked him, hard, heavy muscle encased in satin-soft skin.

A smorgasbord offered up for my hedonistic pleasure.

He groaned, bucked his hips, hands carving through my hair, mad for me. He tasted so fucking good, felt so fucking good.

I caught the onslaught of my spiral, mind and body taking flight.

Gideon shuddered, and I knew I wanted more. More than Sammy. More than this space between us.

"Stop."

A big, strong hand wrapped around his cock and I dropped Sammy beside me.

My gaze clashed with his. "I want you."

He didn't need asking twice. With one swift move he was sheathed, on the bed and into my body.

Bliss.

He growled into my ear. "You're so fucking sexy."

"Ditto."

He grinned. I wrapped my legs around his hips and rode the wave of sensation as his cock pushed me up and over the edge of no return. Fast. Furious. Fucking insane. My flesh pulsed hungrily around him as he thrust one last time, filling my body, feeding my soul.

What had started out as fun had become fan-fucking-tastic. Gideon did that. He made every day different, every time as fresh as the first.

Anticipation skittered through my sex-slaked body. The future opened up, blank pages in my personal biography just waiting to be written. I had a lifetime of firsts to look forward to, starting now.

*G*ideon made it easy to fall into happiness.

Stolen kisses peppered the following days at work, while my nights were heated and hedonistic, Gideon filling my body and feeding my soul, whittling away at the barricades surrounding my heart.

Work in the lab took on a new light. Graeme requested I apply for Mannie's soon-to-be available position. It seemed both Mannie and Gideon were on board with the idea, and that was good enough for him. I bit back the irritation over his willingness to listen to two Y-chromosomes over one pair of X.

Did it really matter how I secured the position? I'd more

than earned it. And now, finally, the promotion was within reach. All it had needed was the belief of one person.

I found myself smiling at the simplest things. Breakfast in bed. A soy latte and choc-berry muffin mysteriously appearing on my desk. Chocolate hearts sprinkled over my pillow. Post-it messages pinned to the refrigerator.

A man's arms around me as I tumbled into sleep, and a firm body cocooning me as I awoke. And sex . . . body-melting, mind-blowing, orgasmic moments that awakened my body and threw every preconceived notion clear out of the water.

So many little things to enrich my world. So easy to become accustomed, to forget what life was like before Gideon.

"Hey."

I looked up from my computer screen and test results the clock told me I'd been staring at blankly for the past fifteen minutes. "Hey." The smile started in my chest before it spread to my lips.

"I was thinking . . ." He leaned in and brushed a curl back from my forehead.

I shivered. "Again? This is becoming a habit."

He moved closer, deliciously filling my space, and all I could smell was pine and Gideon.

"I thought I'd cook dinner tonight. How does paella sound?"

"Fucking fabulous."

"Oh, and I cleared out a drawer." His gaze hooked mine. "Just so you have somewhere to leave your stuff when you stay over."

I froze. It was all happening so fast. *A drawer.* The permanence of those words coiled through my brain.

His brows dipped, his expression etched with concern. "Is one enough? Or do you need two?"

He was so goddam cute, how could I allow my fears to ruin everything we'd built the past few days? I pressed my lips into what I hoped resembled a smile. "One is fine."

"Good." He ducked and dropped a kiss on my nose.

This time the smile was genuine. I swatted him away. "*Gideon!*"

"What? Who's going to say something?" He swept the hair from my neck.

I closed my eyes, his touch playing havoc with the sensitive band of skin beneath my hairline. "It's not what they say, it's what they think. I need to appear professional if I want to be considered for the CDC Head Scientist role."

"Oh, they'll more than consider you if I have anything to do with it."

Emotion thickened in my throat. "Thank you."

"You deserve this, Tiff. You're the best choice for the job."

"That's never mattered before. But this time there's a difference. *You.*"

"This is all on you." The flutter of his fingertips slipped beneath the neckline of my top, sending shivers to the tips of my toes. "But if you insist on thanking me, I can think of a dozen ways."

Heat swamped the flesh between my thighs. "And I can think of a dozen more."

He perched on the edge of my desk, the same desk where he'd delivered that first unforgettable orgasm. Not the disappointment I'd once anticipated.

In fact, nothing about Gideon disappointed.

I scraped my fingernail up the outside of his leg, my blood heating at the glorious way his cock filled his pants.

Fuck.

I'd stopped waiting for that moment. For the bubble to burst and for my spirits to free-fall and crash to the ground. He'd given me no reason to believe he was anything but committed, to me, to us, to the whole Prophesy hoo-ha and spending the rest of our mortal lives together.

The idea wasn't as alarming as it had been in the past. *A lifetime with Gideon.*

It was kinda warming. Kinda cool. Kinda fucking incredible.

30

GIDEON

*I*t was time.

Tiff's body curved perfectly into mine. She fit, so right, so good. I'd woken up, hard as a rock, wanting to sink myself into her heat and leave the world and all its burdens behind.

Then vibrations echoed from my bedside table and I glanced at my cell. *Damon.* His chiseled, taciturn face filled the screen and I knew.

I tamped down my hunger. Time enough to satisfy it when the day was done. Tiff would be in my bed tonight, and every night hereafter. It was destined. The Prophesy didn't lie.

Slowly easing my arm out from under her body, I edged backwards until I met the edge of the bed and slid out from under the covers. A chill hit me with a rush I'd never experienced before now. Or was it the familiarity of Tiff's warmth that made everything feel like ice in comparison?

Dawn was still a couple of hours away, the perfect time to execute our plan undetected.

I dressed, then removed her keycard from her jacket pocket. If the action niggled, I ignored it. I'd be done and back in bed before she stirred, none the wiser. Not that this made my actions any less deplorable. But as I'd been lectured so many times before, *the needs of the many* . . . *blah-di-blah-di-blah.*

Stealth is what I do best, so I made it out the front door with barely a sound. Tiff was still sound asleep, but I walked the bike down half a block before I started the engine just to be sure.

My first stop was Mannie's duplex. I'd long since cut a key after my initial visit, so I entered through the side door. I logged into his computer and tweaked the formula, using the specs Damon had sent across. Then, part one completed, I left the same way I'd entered, ready for part two. I made for the lab.

I was in and out in less than fifteen minutes. On schedule. Twenty minutes more and I'd be home, in bed, losing myself in Tiffany's heat.

Black sky was already transforming to blue and a chorus of trilling woodpeckers heralded the new day. I texted Damon confirmation that the first stage was complete then glanced up from my screen.

My bike was the only vehicle in the far parking lot, but it wasn't alone.

I slipped the keycard into my pocket and tried to look as if I wasn't caught red-handed with my dick swinging in the breeze.

I swallowed, my throat rubbing as dry as the gravel path underfoot. "Tiff."

She stepped forward, arms crossed, shoulders squared, gaze narrowed and fiery, a viper poised and ready to strike.

"Two questions, Gideon, and your answers had better be fan-fucking-tastic." The deepening red on her cheeks screamed one fuse short of an explosion. "Why are you using my keycard to enter a restricted area? And is that the reason you fucked me five ways to Sunday before convincing me to stay on at Hagen?"

31

TIFFANY

*O*ld habits die a hard and painful death.

For as long as I could remember, I'd been cursed with light sleeping—no good could come from forgetting one's surroundings. Self-preservation had made it so.

My inability to sleep through any disturbance, no matter how unobtrusive, had seen me wake the moment Gideon had left the bed. I'd initially assumed he'd return, but when the minutes ran into tens, and his movements seemed more clandestine than considerate, suspicion set in.

Still, even then, I'd chided myself with paranoia.

I'd followed him out the front door in time to watch his motorcycle taillights disappear into the darkness. My investigative activities would have ended there but for one salient fact. He'd taken my keycard.

Only one reason for that.

He wanted access to the lab's restricted areas. Why, I hadn't a clue. All I knew was my blood thundered through my veins and my heart broke a little with each treacherous thought.

Thank fuck for Uber. I called, booked and was on my way to Hagen in less than ten minutes. I arrived first, without a clue where he'd gone on the way, or even if my deduction had been correct. I waited, half hoping I was wrong about him using me to access the lab, the other half wondering where he'd gone instead. Another woman?

I wasn't sure which scenario cut less.

Both were a betrayal, and both demonstrated I'd been duped yet again.

Stupid bitch.

This time the words were mine, not Richard's.

*W*hat the fuck, Gideon?"

He stood, palms open, my frigging stolen keycard in his jacket pocket. "I can explain."

"It better be fucking good." His sudden blink and the shutter in his expression made me add, "And it better be fucking true."

He strode forwards, reaching out for my arm. I wrenched back. I didn't want his touch. I wasn't sure I'd ever want it again.

Something in my heart splintered. The one piece the past few days had managed to make whole again.

He scrubbed the back of his neck and I didn't want to notice the play of muscles beneath his tee. Muscles I'd owned and enjoyed, thinking I'd own and enjoy them through years beyond now.

"Let's go somewhere private."

"Let's not." I stepped back, just in case he thought me standing there was an invitation for him to join me. "Tell me what's so goddam important you had to screw me and spurn all that *'truth and honor abound'* bullshit."

He scanned the area, all Jason Bourne and conspiracy theory like. "I can't do this here. It's not secure." His gaze looked so destroyed, as if he were the one who'd been betrayed.

What the fuck?

"Give me one good reason why I should trust anything you say."

"Because what I'm doing is so damned important I'd risk my mortality and even my life."

A ten ton boulder slammed me full in the chest.

Heartstrings that had seen me blunder in the past pulled me back under their spell. Why did I find it so impossible to harden my heart against this man? How did I know, even now, if the words spilling from his lips were true?

Short answer—I didn't.

But I had to trust something. Perhaps the past few days and the feelings he'd stirred up inside me, feelings he'd seemed to return. Unless they were all lies, too.

My head spun, belief and doubt swirling with equal confusion about my brain. Whatever the outcome, I had to *know*.

I shrugged, as if this whole situation wasn't devastating the world he'd made me believe was possible. "Fine."

The absence of that cocky, all-knowing smile was enough to hint my tentative trust may not be unfounded.

He sidestepped past, handing me my helmet before putting on his. The irony hit me. "Why do you wear a helmet?"

"It's the law."

Of course. It wasn't as if the colored polycarbonate and foam could save him. Only I could do that.

Was even that true?

Something deep inside me said it was. Perhaps it was the vision, or a connection between us I seemed unable to shake. But when he said we were fated to be together, everything else in my life made sense.

Until he'd lied and used me, that is.

Just a small fucking wrench in the works.

Much as the last thing I wanted was to be plastered against the lying bastard, I followed him onto his bike, steeling myself as I wrapped my arms around his torso. I pulled his betrayal front-center to my thoughts and held it there, a barrier between him and my body's need to sink into him.

That whole prophesy hoo-ha wielded some strong voodoo shit, because my mind screamed even while my heart twisted and hammered at our close proximity.

I'd been so deep in my thoughts, I didn't realize where he'd taken me until the large white sign appeared before us.

No fucking way.

By the time my mind computed, he'd already stopped and was engaging the Harley's kickstand. I jumped off and away from the memories, sudden cold slicing deep into my bones. He'd forever ruined my sanctuary and I resented the crap out of him for it.

The brook bubbled in the distance, failing to provide its usual sense of peace. Even the birdsong welcoming dawn failed to chip at the tension in my spine.

I waved my hand in his direction, trying to stem a shivering that cut me deep to the core. "Talk."

He nodded, still astride his monster of a machine. "Promise you won't breathe a word to anyone."

Was he fucking kidding?

The oak's gnarly heart taunted me. *Fool me once . . .*

"I'm not promising shit. Not when I have no fucking idea what that promise means."

32

GIDEON

I was a stick of gum stretched one tug shy of snapping.

What the fuck was I supposed to do?

Come clean and put the lives of my coven, my entire kind, at risk? Or maintain my silence and lose my one chance for a normal life, and worse, my chance for love.

Time froze. My thoughts spiraling backwards two hundred years past and a decision that forever marked me. I'd trusted a woman, and others had suffered for my mistake. I'd vowed never to risk that kind of trust again.

Our mission, modifying the antidote, hurt no one and saved more lives than any one man could count. It was bigger than me, than Tiff, than our fated futures.

I had to believe that.

I left the bike to breach the distance between us. "I can't tell you what I was doing or why, but I can tell you it's for the better good."

"What the hell is that supposed to mean?"

"I need you to trust me."

She laughed then. An empty, mirthless laugh that fell far short of her heart. "You ask me for trust but won't trust me back."

"I . . ." I scrubbed the back of my neck, doing nothing to unravel the kinks. "I can't."

"You want something for nothing. That's not how the world works, Gideon. You, of all people, should know that."

"This isn't my secret to tell."

"Then whose is it?"

I wanted to give her something, but how could I? Impossible to know where safety ended and consequences began.

"Things are going to happen in the next few days, and they're going to seem bad. I need you to know that what I've done is for the good of more than just vamps. It benefits you too."

"But you can't tell me what."

"No."

"Yet you want me to trust you. Blindly."

"Yes."

"You're so full of bull." I almost growled. "Trust you, my ass. Take me back."

"We should talk about this."

"That's your answer to everything, isn't it? You talk, I listen, you convince, I foolishly believe. That's not the way this goes from now on." Her teeth gritted so tight I could hear the grind of enamel against enamel. "Take. Me. Back."

I stepped forward, nostrils flaring. She wrapped her arms around her torso and stumbled back, shivering as if the cold in my blood had invaded hers.

The sight made me want to yell and rage and curse a world that seemed determined to destroy me.

I returned to the motorcycle, holding out the helmet for her to take. She snatched it from my hands, then stepped away, as if I were poison. Then she carefully mounted. Her stiff, detached hold around my waist chilled my already cold blood. So different from the previous, warm wrap of her arms.

I took her straight home. She was quite clear about that. And in terms of her drawer and its contents back at my place, she was unequivocal—toss them into a box and drop them into her office at work, preferably when she wasn't around.

Subtext—if I see your ass any time this millennium, it'll be too soon.

I walked her safely to her front door, despite her protests, then watched her disappear, the sharp turn of her lock severing the final link between us. Slashing my last hopes of mortality and escaping what my very mission sought to prevent.

﹌

The lab was in chaos.

The mission had gone as planned. Damon had already called to voice his pleasure and inform me that global destruction of the serum antidote had been a success. The cold storage failure had done its job.

The only remaining original antidote was stored under lock and key, back at the coven's lab.

I hadn't shared that I'd been caught in the act by Tiff. I know what his next order would have been and I wasn't about to eliminate a threat I didn't believe existed.

Graeme paced the corridor, angst oozing out from his

shoulders and his blistering glower. He railed at Mannie, who in turn railed at anyone who would listen. The room had been serviced only a month previously. What could possibly have caused it and the generator backup to fail? And not only fail—the room had heated to the point of denaturation, rendering every sample inside useless. A short circuit in the security system made it impossible to determine whose keycard had last accessed the room. It had to be human error.

Close, but not close enough.

"A fucking mess." Graeme waved a pudgy arm towards Mannie. "Call WHO and beg off some of their serum." With a huff, he stormed off in the direction of his office, leaving a bunch of lab techs to dispose of the spoiled samples.

I felt no guilt. Perhaps heads would roll, but more likely —once they discovered the global destruction—blame would fall as it had in the past. Peace of Nature was the perfect foil. The group had protested vigorously against the antidote's airborne release, arguing the potential for unforeseen side effects on wildlife, as well as the environment as a whole.

They weren't far wrong.

Despite the bedlam overtaking the lab, it was Tiff's gaze I sought.

Her glare hurled daggers and they hit their mark, straight through the place where my beating heart would have been.

She had to suspect the cold storage malfunction was my work, yet she hadn't shared her intel. Not yet. I had to hope she'd continue her silence.

What I did discover, through another of Graeme's rants, was she'd withdrawn her application for Head Scientist. I was thankful she hadn't tendered her resignation at the same time.

Maybe that was more about timing than her desire to stay on in a laboratory with me.

I tried a grin, which probably translated as a sort of a twist, and tossed her a light "Hi."

She nodded then turned her back. She may as well have whacked me with a baseball bat. Her cheeks were flushed, her gaze glossy, as if she tottered on the brink of tears. I did that, and every fiber of my being wanted to take it back.

There were too many all-seeing eyes around for me to say more. And in reality, what could I say? The only way out of this animosity was to tell her the truth, and that was something I couldn't do. Not while there was still room for the mission to crash.

I trudged back to Mannie's office and prepared to further my deception with offers of help and support.

For decades I'd maintained a distance from those around me. Detachment was easier than suffering the wrench each time I left with no word, no trace. I'd believed I was prepared for all this mission entailed, but time had dulled the memories, and the consequence of getting too close. Of using and hurting people I'd come to call friends.

I may not brandish a live, beating heart, but I still hurt as readily as any normal living man.

33

TIFFANY

*S*o much for an invigorating bike ride to clear my head.

The heavens had waited until I was halfway home before they opened up and unleashed. Too far from the lab to turn back. Too far from home to escape the downpour. I was so wet, it was useless to even think about stopping to don my jacket.

I ducked my head—at least that way the rain dripped off my helmet and onto my handlebars—and peddled faster. A two mile ride and I was only one mile from warmth and dry clothes.

The road was quiet, only a trickle of traffic slicing through puddles and spraying water up my legs, soaking my thighs.

Wet is wet. You can't get any wetter, right?

A perfect end to a perfect day.

Gideon fucking Fang. Trouble since the day he'd waltzed into our frigging strategy meeting, then just as easily waltzed into my heart.

Yeah, his betrayal sucked. He'd made me care, then cut at emotions I'd previously kept buried beneath a veneer of control.

I knew he'd tampered with not only the cold storage, but the backup generator as well. And he'd used my keycard to do it. I just didn't know why.

And until I knew the answer to that question, how could I come clean? I was complicit—I'd fucking slept with the guy, giving him free and easy access to my keycard, to any and every avenue of access I had to the lab.

Somewhere in the far recesses of my heart, I hoped whatever his reasons, he hadn't been lying. That his actions were, as he'd promised, for the greater good. Although how allowing the spread of a virus that threatened pandemic proportions could be termed "good" escaped me.

Another vehicle approached, and I swerved as close to the berm of the road as I dared. Wet or not, at least it would lessen the spray.

The surrounding road glistened gold with headlights that seemed determined to remain abreast rather than passing. An engine gunned.

"Tiff!"

Even with the roar of wind and rain in my ears, I heard the voice. Warmth fluttered deep in my gut, fanning out until my blood burned. Ridiculous when my skin was like ice and I was still fucking furious at the deceitful bastard. It seemed my body was still to come to the "I'd been burned again" party, instead of remaining under Gideon's orgasmic frigging spell.

Freaking typical.

I ducked my head, lower still. Maybe if I ignored him long enough, he'd give up and go away.

"Tiff!"

Fat chance. The man made mules look meek. Since when had he ever given up? Particularly when it came to me and saving his firm, fucking ass.

I waved my hand in an unequivocal "piss off" gesture and kept peddling. I obviously needed my head examined if I thought he'd take the hint.

"Don't be ridiculous, Tiff. Pull over."

The motorcycle pulled up beside me. He wasn't going away, and I couldn't concentrate with him right there, legs spread-eagled across that great machine. I hit the brakes. The tires squealed, wheels skidding over the loose gravel. The bike flipped, tossing my body like a frigging cannonball, up and over the handlebars. For a few glorious, heart-stopping moments I flew through the air, weightless, free, then the road and my body met with an almighty slam.

Fuck.

The world swam, but that didn't stop his voice from permeating the cloud and dancing on the edge of consciousness. I wanted him gone, and I told him so, in mutters that were totally incomprehensible to anyone but me.

I felt his hands on my body, methodically checking for injury. I knew enough to know the pain I felt wasn't from broken bones. My entire right side would be black with bruises in the morning. I'd have a whopper of a headache, and sharp pain every time I put one foot in front of the other.

Then there was my heart . . .

He released the straps on my helmet and eased it off.

The shivers that had slowly deepened over the past few days, intensified.

"Moja láska, I've got you." He wrapped me in his arms and lifted me as if he were lifting feathers. Warmth spilled

around me, combating the cold biting through my skin. I should have pulled away—if I'd been sensible, that's exactly what I would have done—but something dragged me in. I pushed my face into the wool of his sweater and blocked out the world and everything that said he and I were wrong.

Right now, this feeling, me in his arms, it didn't feel wrong. It felt . . . *warm*.

And I was. So. *So*. Cold.

Tired.

He eased me onto the bike, my legs either side, my body pressed tightly against his as he wrapped his arms around me once more. "Let's get you home, *moja láska.*"

Again, those words. I had no clue of their meaning, but they sounded as warm as his sweater and as comforting as his large, muscular frame shielding me from the storm.

That he'd lied to me and used me seemed to register less than my need for warmth.

The engine gunned, and the bike lurched forward. His grip tightened and cold air rushed past, so fast, as if the world raced by us with lightning speed. Of course, it wasn't possible. But through the fuzziness engulfing my brain, that's how it felt.

My body began to shiver. It wouldn't stop, no matter how much I willed it. I scrunched my eyes closed and let my body meld into his. Wishing I could go back in time, to those moments when I thought my visions formed part of The Prophesy instead of a plan to taunt me with what I could never, would never, have.

34

GIDEON

I'd fucked up royally and now Tiff was suffering the consequences.

Clammy skin. Face flushed red. Feverish and barely conscious. My medical training kicked in as I perched on the edge of her bed and assessed her temperature before checking the responsiveness of her pupils.

Over three hundred years I'd gathered multiple professions, general medicine being just one. You never knew when you'd need to call on that knowledge. Like now.

The force of her reaction wasn't from the fall. This was something else. A virus, maybe?

A chill washed my body. Not *the* virus?

I tucked the blankets tighter round her shivering torso and daubed a damp cloth across her brow. Her head rolled to one side, then the next, a trail of nonsensible gibberish unleashing from her lips.

"Shhh." I brushed my lips to hers. Perhaps the contact would stem the flow and settle her restlessness somehow.

The ramblings intensified. Then nonsense mumblings

transformed into clear, panicked cries. *"No!"*

I brushed back a clump of sweat-soaked hair and this time kissed her brow. *"Shhh."*

She shrank away from my touch. *"Stop. Please stop."* She wrestled with the blankets, slamming a wild fist into my chin when I leaned in to help. I rolled my jaw, tasted blood. Mine.

Again her head rolled to the side. Her nostrils quivered. She whimpered, her voice barely discernable, but I heard all the same. *"So much blood."*

She shuddered, then turned onto her side, curling up into a tight, trembling ball.

I wanted to kill that bastard Richard, with every fiber of my being.

She barely registered when I straightened the covers this time. Jerky breaths wrenched sharp and shallow through her pale lips, and with each one my mouth dried a little more. How could the virus have hit so fast?

Not that the *how* made any difference. I couldn't keep her in my home when she needed full medical treatment that only a hospital could provide. I called 911, even while my mind spun with the knowledge that if needed, production of the new serum was still days away.

I could only hope that my hunch was way off and she'd suffered from no more than a knock to the head and a simple, everyday Rhinovirus-based common cold.

I've always hated the cloying of disinfectant at the back of my throat almost as much as I hated a hospital's sterile, white-washed walls and the resonant disharmony of heart monitors.

Two days had passed since Tiff flew off her bike and into a fever-induced haze. My fears had been founded the moment her blood test results came back—Influenza A H3N2v4, the variant flu virus for which the serum had been designed to stop.

No other known cure existed once the infection took hold.

Tiff had no next of kin in Louisiana, and I hadn't realized the extent of Richard's alienation tactics till I'd seen the consequences for myself. No friends had contacted the lab or called her cell since she'd been admitted.

No one seemed to care whether she lived or died.

Bar one. I alternated between vigils at her bedside and visiting the lab, helping Graeme restock and reinstate all the necessary samples for Hagen to function. All the while I waited for my next contact from Damon, bracing each time my cell pealed.

I heard the soft swish of the formidable Nurse Wright's scrubs long before she entered the room and spoke. "Still here?"

I nodded and spared her a smile.

Where else would I go? It wasn't as if I needed the sleep craved by mortals. I would have looked fresh, as if just arrived from the required eight hours, if not for the crumple of my days old shirt and jeans.

She took it all in, mistaking my tired attire for fatigue. "You should get some rest."

"I will when she's out of danger."

Deep, weather-beaten lines cut deeper still into her face. I hated the pity I saw there as much as I hated the pain it wielded.

"Ahh, Doctor."

We both turned as Doc Huang walked through the door in his signature pristine white coat and black jeans. He made for the head of the bed, grabbed the clipboard and flipped through the top few pages.

I saw the same look of puzzlement I'd seen in Nurse Wright every time she checked Tiff's vitals. The same defeat.

"Her temperature's spiked again. Keep pushing the fluids and let's up the antivirals." He nudged back his black-rimmed glasses, then scrawled on the top page before returning the board to the bed.

I unclasped Tiff's clammy hand and stood up. "What's the prognosis, Doc?"

He scrutinized me through his circular lenses the way he'd scrutinized me every time I'd asked that same question over the past two days. "At the moment, we're working to break her fever."

"What about killing the virus?"

"For that we need the antidote. Not sure if you've been following the media, but worldwide stocks have been destroyed. We're waiting for the new batch, but that's still days off."

Not news to me. I'd never felt so goddam helpless. "Will she be okay until then?" I asked the question all the while knowing the answer. That I hoped for something different was just plain fucking stupid.

"Her rising temperature is a concern. If we can stabilize it, she'll have a chance."

"And if not?"

"I'd suggest you contact any family and friends. It might pay for them to visit sooner rather than later."

He didn't need to add that the visit was for farewells and not for support.

"What if she had access to the antidote today?"

"There's never any guarantee, but her chances would be greatly increased." His look lacked the nurse's pity, that whole reserved medical bedside manner firmly back in its place. "Unfortunately, that's not an option here."

Maybe as far as the doc was concerned, but I knew different.

I'd known Damon for as long as I'd been a vamp. We'd been friends once. The best of. Then I'd fucked up and things had splintered between us, transforming our relationship into less than friends, more than acquaintances.

Once upon a time, I'd have laid all my cards on the table and Damon would have picked them up without batting an eye. Those days were long gone, which meant if I wanted to save Tiff, I was about to betray my oldest once-upon-a-time friend.

I pushed through the front door of Uncle Sam's Souvenirs and headed for the kid behind the counter.

"Hey, Marco. Is he in?"

He raised his brown-black gaze from the flashing screen in his hand—no doubt the latest video game craze sweeping the teen population—and shook his head. "Nah, he's out for lunch."

"Aaron?"

"With him."

"I need to check on something. Let me through?"

He barely blinked. I'd always come and gone as I pleased. There was no reason for Marco to believe today was any different than those countless other occasions.

I entered the four digit passcode into the keypad to the right of the counter, then pushed through the blue painted door. I passed the rows of shelving and stock to reach the innocuous door at the far end. This time a six digit code released the lock.

I pushed inside and entered the bright-lit corridor. The offices were to my right, the labs to my left. It took me less than five minutes to enter and leave the lab with just one vial of the antidote secreted in my jacket pocket.

"Gideon."

I looked up to see the two people I'd hoped to avoid. Damon stopped, barring my exit, and puppy dog Aaron followed suit.

I dredged up a smile. "Hey, guys."

Damon's scrutiny swept from head to toe and I knew he'd registered every detail in that one foul look. "What brings you here?"

"Wanted to see if you were free for lunch."

His steely grey gaze narrowed. "We've just been."

"Damn. Maybe next time then?" I made to pass.

"Doesn't mean we can't catch up." He nodded to Aaron, who faded into the background like the good little PA he was. "Come into my office."

Come into my parlor . . .

Yeah, I wasn't stupid. Damon's *invitation* had nothing to do with an innocent catch up. We hadn't "caught up" as friends since 1735.

I didn't need this shit. Time was ticking and Tiff needed

the antidote, fast. I resisted the urge to check my pocket. Good old Eagle Eyes would notice immediately.

We climbed a set of narrow stairs and then entered the large, light room that was our coven leader's office. He bypassed the couches and made for the impressive ergonomic throne behind three thousand pounds of nineteenth century Victorian mahogany.

Arms resting on his prize desk, he waved towards the upright chair opposite, and it would have been churlish—and foolish—for me not to take it. "Nice lunch?"

He continued to stare until unease turned to apprehension. What the fuck did he know?

Elbows perched on the rests either side of my chair, I tented my fingers in the center and waited, returning his gaze to show I had nothing to hide.

Finally, he relaxed back, his scrutiny no less severe. "How's it all going?"

"As planned."

"Not the mission. You."

He was starting to wangle into my nerves. Biting the bullet seemed better than being bitten myself. "We know you don't give a shit how I am, so cut the bull and tell me what this is really about."

I might just as well have slapped the superiority from his supercilious face. It was the first time either one of us had voiced what lurked beneath the pretext of our old and over *friendship*.

"Is there anything I should know that could compromise the mission at this point?"

I looked him right in the eyes. "No."

"So, that girl, Tiffany, sick and in hospital isn't a problem?"

"Not for the mission."

"But it is for you?"

"Well, yeah. I'd kinda like it if she didn't die." The words may have sounded casual, but they cut like a stake through my soul.

"What does she mean to you?"

"I care what happens."

"And that's all?"

"What more could there be?"

Again that squint. Again the scrutiny.

Fuck if it wasn't making me squirm.

"So, we're not staring at another Annaline episode?"

I shook my head. A woman I'd loved had screwed me and betrayed the coven, and the entire situation had been relegated to an *episode*. Like forty minutes of some lame TV soap opera.

I bit my tongue and every angry word that would push Damon more offside. It happened over two hundred years ago for fuck's sake. I'd been wrong, he'd been right, end of story. Why couldn't the bastard forget and move on?

"Do I need to remind you that people died the last time you followed your dick."

"It seems you do, every chance you get."

"Don't be an ass."

"My thoughts exactly." I pushed forward. "If there's nothing else? Much as this meander down memory lane has been a blast, I have a job to get back to."

"Of course." He sighed, scrubbing his hand through stubby, dark blond hair. "You know I only want what's best for all of us. The coven, you, me. Sometimes that means making the hard choices."

"I didn't deliberately fall for the wrong girl. Just like I didn't deliberately trust the wrong guy."

"I saved our people. It wouldn't kill you to be grateful once in a while."

"Oh, I am. Because hanging me out to dry was a necessary part of your whole superhero saving the world production, right?"

"I can't talk to you like this, Gideon."

"At last, something we agree on." I slapped my palm on the over-polished desktop. "Are we done?"

"Yeah."

Finally. I was out of my chair and at the door before one second had ticked over to the next.

"Before you go."

I turned, so close I could feel the brush of freedom beyond the solid wood.

"Turn out your pockets."

My hand dropped from the doorknob. "What?"

"Turn. Out. Your. Pockets."

"Why?" I measured the distance between us. I wouldn't make it. He was always faster than I. Faster. Stronger. Better.

Until Annaline.

He stood and skirted the desk. "Do you really want to do this?"

"Do what? Leave?" I clenched and unclenched my fist. What I'd do to deck the bastard. "Is it so goddam hard for you to trust me, Damon? Fuck man. It was two fucking centuries ago. What the hell have I done since to earn the constant cynicism?"

"When were you going to tell me this Tiffany is your soulmate?"

216

The room began to spin like one of those playground roundabouts. My throat rasped. "How'd you guess?"

"The mark is on her neck, for chrissake." If I thought he still cared an ounce for me, I would have believed the break in his voice for hurt. It had to be anger. Deep, dark, centuries-old. Unforgiving. Anger.

It suddenly clicked. "Nurse Wright."

"You know we have people everywhere."

It was true. But usually I was in the know. That I wasn't this time was just another slash to our already dead and buried friendship.

"Thanks for the faith, old friend."

He barely flinched. The taciturn in his expression deepened frown-lines that seemed to come hand-in-hand with his span of leadership. "It's not about faith, and it's not personal. It's about ensuring the mission. Saving our people and saving everyone around us. That includes your Tiffany."

"I'm all for the mission and saving the world."

"So empty your pockets, then you can get back to it."

I considered running, or whipping his holier-than-thou ass. His finger poised over a button under his desk. One press and Aaron would come running with a whole host of others.

No way out of this corner.

I slipped my hand into my pocket and my fingertips encountered the smooth vial still cold from storage. I placed it carefully on the desk in front of him. "Happy?"

I didn't wait for an answer. I didn't particularly care.

I'd failed. Tiffany was lying in that god-awful hospital, fighting for her life, and I couldn't do a goddam thing about it.

35

TIFFANY

*H*azy fog thickened my world.

Shallow breaths wheezed thinly out from my lungs, thick and dense with the slump of wet cement. My throat burned.

I struggled to unplaster my eyelids. *So damned heavy.* It hurt. Even the smallest movement seemed impossible.

Instead, I lay beneath something over-starched and scratchy, and listened. I was in a hospital room. The rhythmic beep of a heart monitor and the residual reek of overcooked fat and mashed potatoes was a dead giveaway.

How long had I been here?

My entire body blazed, sticky, sweaty. All but my left hand. I centered my thoughts there, where it felt cool and comfortable. I dragged open one eyelid, enough to see Gideon slumped in a chair beside me, his hand tightly wrapped in mine.

Strange. I'd floated in and out of consciousness over the past however long, and each time he'd featured in what I'd believed to be visions. His hand in mine didn't feel like a vision, it felt solid, real, reliable.

My brain was a rambling, roiling tumult—a snow globe filled with words and ideas that had been shaken nonsensically.

I tried to focus on how I felt about Gideon, how I felt about his lies. The anger wouldn't come. All I felt was relief that he was here, for me.

I'd never experienced that kind of dependability, not since Mom died. I relied on no one—me, myself and I formed my whole world. Things had worked just fine, until I glimpsed what it was to have someone in my corner.

No longer did I have to go it alone. It felt good. Even if the feeling had been fleeting. Time with Gideon was filled with so much good, surely it wasn't all lies?

"Tiff."

His cool breath fanned my cheek and it felt amazing.

I stirred and managed to crank open a second eye. Another breath shuddered through my lips. *So dry.*

I tried to speak. *No sound.*

Cool and wet brushed my lips. A cloth. Then it swept my brow. I recalled vague memories of the same sensation, many times over. Was that too Gideon?

He stroked my brow. "You need to fight this, Tiff. I don't want to lose you."

Of course he didn't. Because that meant he'd lose his mortality.

I hated that my mind went there, but much as I craved the life his bite and the visions promised, I had to hold what was real at the forefront of my mind. If I lost myself in a dream that turned to dust, how would I drag my way back from the disappointment?

Something caught in my throat. I tried to breathe. Tried to cough past the boulder blocking oxygen to my body.

He propped me up, rubbing my back, whispering words I couldn't quite comprehend. The words I'd heard over and over through the interminable fog.

"Moja láska."

Somehow they gave me comfort, when my thoughts would see me drown.

The coughing subsided, leaving my body weak, my breathing a mere whisper of what it was. That same cool, wet cloth returned, moistening my lips, releasing drops of refreshing liquid that softened the sandpaper lining my throat.

The cloth swept down my neck, down one arm, the next, momentarily stifling the burn. Ease seeped into my body. A sea, soft rolling waves lulling me into peace.

The cloth stiffened. Stopped. "What the fuck are you doing here, Damon?" The frost in Gideon's voice cut through my haze.

"Much as you seem determined to believe it, I don't hate you, Gideon."

"Give the man an Oscar, because you sure hide it well."

A sigh. Not Gideon's. "I came to see if you need anything."

"Other than the antidote, no."

Another sigh. "I wish we could move past this crap." A pause. "I hate that Annaline used you and betrayed us, that she carved up our friendship and spat it out like sour milk. And even more, I hate that she's still here, still weaving her spells and shitting all over whatever we have left."

"This is nothing like what happened with Annaline."

"Maybe. But you're making life-altering decisions over a girl you barely know."

"I'm not the green adolescent I was back then. I know enough."

The exchange washed over me, turbulent, unsettling.

My eyes fluttered open just seconds before nausea hit. But I'd seen enough. A tall, grim-faced man stepped further into the room, black clothing, light hair, dark, angry eyes.

"If I were to hand over the antidote, have you thought about what happens once the serum enters her blood? You can never bond. You can never be mortal. If her blood ever enters yours, it'll be no different from the disaster we've just prevented. The antidote will spark The Change and we'll be forced to hunt you down." A sigh, the scrape of a hand through hair. "You may save her, Gideon, but by doing so, your one chance for mortality, or any remaining immortality, will be gone. How can I call myself a friend if I stand by and let you throw your entire existence away?"

The silence following that little IED stretched for the longest time.

I'd thought the pain in my body unbearable, the rasp of every breath interminable, but nothing matched the puncture of those words to my heart. At first I'd agreed to bond with Gideon to save him, and somehow save myself. But somewhere along the way, something had changed. I'd clutched onto the image of our shared future, and thoughts of it disappearing made my already ragged breath catch.

"I love her, Damon."

All doubts left me with the crack in Gideon's voice and those four wondrous words as they wrenched from his throat.

Fuck.

"Fuck." The other voice—Gideon's frenemy—his reaction mirroring mine.

"I was afraid you'd say that." Rustling. Then frenemy's voice again. "Here. We destroyed the other vials, but I couldn't destroy them all knowing I'd lose you altogether."

A sharp breath. A step. "What's the catch?"

"No catch. I just want my old friend back." A pause. "Save her Gideon."

Silence. Then the swish of fabric. A hug? Backslapping.

Cool hands freed my arm from the covers and ice-cold swabbed the inside of my elbow.

The reality of what Gideon was about to do hit me square in the chest.

No!

I pulled away, trying to free my arm. *"Stop."* The word hissed through my parched lips. I shook my head, setting off a spinning that refused to let up.

"Tiff." His cool palm brushed my brow. Cold until I could make it warm. "I have the antidote. You need to hold still."

"No." I dragged in a shallow breath. "You won't . . . be mortal."

"That doesn't matter."

"Do it now." He raised the syringe and I shrunk back. "Not . . . that. The mating."

Horror filled his expression. "No way. It's too risky. You're too weak. You need this Tiff. Trust me."

Funny thing was, I finally did. Too fucking late to matter.

"My blood . . . poison . . . you." Even as I said the words, bile scoured my burning throat. Coughing wracked my body. He raised me again, rubbing my back, caring for me in a way I'd never been cared for before.

How could I lose him? Not when I'd only now discovered the truth.

Love was more than manipulation. It was sacrifice.

I tried to tell him. To let him know he should take me before it was too late. But the fog had thickened. The sandpaper in my throat swelled. I gulped, drowning, gasping for breath that totally evaded me. My mouth opened, but dark talons dragged me under.

This wasn't the end. It wasn't the vision. We were meant for each other. *Two marks make one, two hearts made whole.*

How could he not see?

Life would be meaningless if I had to live it without him.

36

GIDEON

"*D*amon!"

My old friend moved in. He checked Tiff's pulse, pulled back her lids to check her pupils. "She's still alive."

Barely.

I readied the syringe. "Hold her arm."

"Are you sure?"

I glanced at him then. "What would you do?"

He barely hesitated. His long lean fingers wrapped the tourniquet firmly around Tiff's bicep and tugged it tight.

"Wait." He closed the door, wedging a chair beneath the handle, then grabbed a pair of gloves from the dispenser and dropped them onto the bed. "Put them on."

I didn't argue. There wasn't time. I slid them on, then tapped for a vein, feeling the weak throb of Tiff's blood beneath my fingertip, the barely there flow drying the back of my throat. I inserted the needle then caught the vein, releasing the tourniquet, holding steady as I slowly injected the serum.

The antidote was meant to be fast acting, but I had no idea what that meant in terms of time and Tiff's situation. Surely fate wouldn't fuck me over this. I couldn't be too late.

I withdrew the needle, stemming the blood with cotton wool and tape, tossing my gloves and the empty syringe into the bright yellow bin.

I nudged Damon aside, dropping into a chair, gripping Tiff's hand, rubbing her knuckles. Maybe if I rubbed hard enough, I could rub the life back into her blood.

An age passed, nothing changed. The rhythmic *tick* of a clock raced the turmoil of my thoughts. My thumb continued its play over her knuckles.

Surely this wasn't it.

Her eyes shot open.

My grip tightened.

She gasped, her skin suddenly cooler, less clammy. Rosy, not feverish red.

The fever had broken.

Thank God.

Another gasp. *Mine.* My hand dropped.

Fuck!

My chest constricted.

Tiff inhaled, each breath sucking air from my lungs as if through a straw. I staggered up from my seat, a twisting, burning, splintering in my chest. Like a stake, piercing the place that should have housed my heart. A heart that would never beat, never live, never love.

But Tiff was saved. *Alive.* That was all that mattered.

"Gideon." Damon. Shock filled his expression. "Fuck!"

I lurched. He grabbed my arms, my legs crumpled. Droning sirens battered against my eardrums. My head spun.

Tiff screamed. Another pierce to my chest. I tried to speak. No sound. No breath. No words.

My eyes rolled back in my head, darkness drowning my world. Stealing my last breath before I was no more.

37

TIFFANY

*N*oooo!
        Pain ripped through my chest.

I pushed up in time to see Gideon crumple to the floor.

"What have you done?" I looked from Frenemy to Gideon, then to the hole in my arm where the antidote had entered.

I couldn't save him now. Nobody could save him.

But he should still have been alive. Immortal. Or had I robbed him of that too?

No-no no-no no-no noooo.

I slid off the bed, shaky, shivering, dropping to my knees. My fingers fluttered across his face, his chest, wrapping his hands in mine, bringing them to my lips.

So very cold. The way he'd been in life.

Would he warm now that he was no longer?

Tears spilled from my face, wetting his cheeks, spotting the crumpled gray of his shirt. His eyes were open but empty. His chest still. Silent.

"Gideon."

I rubbed his hands, holding them to my heart, as if the beat in mine could somehow inject a beat into his.

Stupid. So stupid.

I should have told him. I should have known. Through all my mistakes, this was the one I'd never forgive.

I pressed my lips to his. A fairytale kiss. All I needed was a fairytale ending. The vision I'd wanted with all my heart that would never, could never, come true. Not now. Not ever.

"Gideon."

I kissed his face, his chin. His beautiful, strong neck. Then I returned to his lips.

"Don't die. Please don't die." I kissed him again. If only I could breathe life into his lungs. "Don't die. Not now. Not when you have so much to live for." I kissed his lips, salty tears mingling with a taste I would never forget. "Not when I love you."

Sharp pain zapped my palms.

I pulled back.

Another zap, shooting up my arms as if I'd touched electric wire.

I dropped his hands.

He gasped.

I scrambled backwards as his body arched up on heels and head, suspending his torso clear off the floor like some frigging supernatural possession shit.

Fuck!

He collapsed on another gasp. A dry, desperate, oxygen-starved drag for air.

I crawled back, grabbing his hands once more. *Warm. Yielding.*

His eyes shot open. Beautiful twin forests that latched onto mine.

My heart stuttered. "Gideon!"

His lips parted and I kissed them, so warm, so alive.

He kissed me back, his hands raking my hair, devouring me as if I were his life source.

I wanted that so much.

We broke for air and he pushed up. I straddled his hips and cupped his magnificent face. "I thought I'd lost you."

"I needed you to live." He covered my hands and warmth flooded them.

"Not without you." I shook my head, tears spilling freely over my nose, my chin. "I was stupid."

"You were justified."

"I love you."

He grinned his glorious, heart-stopping grin. "That's the best thing I've heard all day."

I kissed him then. With all my heart. With all my soul.

I had my dream and nothing else mattered.

A-hem.

We broke free. Turned. *Frenemy.*

"Damon."

Frenemy moved in then, when before he'd given us space. "That was one fucking A-rated display you put on, bro."

Gideon grinned again, and it was the most beautiful sight I'd ever seen. "It's been an age since you called me that."

Frenemy rubbed his chin and grinned back. "It's been an age since I was sure it wouldn't trigger another crack to the jaw."

A look passed between them. A look that had to span centuries.

Gideon swallowed. "Thanks, bro."

"Anytime." Frenemy tilted his head towards the door. "Think we should let them in?"

It was only then I heard the banging and bellowing of voices outside.

I clambered off Gideon and Frenemy helped him up. The men hugged, backslapped, did all that macho man-bonding that men do, then Gideon took my hand and squeezed. "Ready?"

I looked up into his face, beautiful and flushed red with the flow of life through his veins. "Always."

Then Frenemy opened the door.

38

TIFFANY

"*B*est. Meal. *Ever.*" I dropped my fork onto my empty plate, not a speck remaining of the feast Gideon had painstakingly prepared for my welcome home—roasted lime chicken breast with a fresh salsa of cherry and avocado in a lime and olive oil dressing. I licked my oil-coated lips.

His gaze tracked my tongue's path, eyes darkening to brilliant, deep-ocean green—the glowing vampire gold forever relegated to the past.

I loved his reaction. Loved that his hunger for me hadn't waned with his newly found mortality. If anything, it had grown.

I swirled the pale pink cider in my glass then sipped. A medley of apple, cranberry and basil tripped across my tongue. "I've been thinking."

His gorgeous lips dipped into the lethal slide of a grin. "A dangerous preoccupation."

I tipped my head. "Touché."

I returned my glass to the table and snagged a cherry and

chunk of avocado from Gideon's plate. "I think I've figured out how your mortal transformation occurred without The Prophesy's whole *love and essence combine* scenario."

He dropped his elbows to the table and leaned in. "I'm all ears."

He was more than that, but for once I didn't feel the need to avoid conversation or our connection with sex. This moment, talking and sharing, filled my soul in a way fucking never had. That didn't mean sex was relegated to the shelf, only that it was sidelined. For now.

"Surrender heart, body and soul. That's sacrifice, right? You willingly sacrificed it all. Your mortality. For me. Maybe that's how you were saved."

"Maybe." He thoughtfully knocked back a mouthful of lager, contemplating the gold and black label as he swallowed. "It doesn't explain one thing, though."

I sipped my wine, wracking my brains. We'd discussed Gideon's change in detail on the way home, after, all through his preparation of dinner, agreeing that what had taken place back in the hospital made sense but for one salient factor— we'd never performed the whole exchange essence and bite ritual. As it turned out, sacrifice trumped sex. But everything else added up, so… "What did we miss?"

He grinned, eyes glinting. "How does Sammy fit into all of this?"

Laughter burst from my lips, along with a generous serving of wine. I grabbed a napkin and mopped up my plate. "He's an old friend."

"So, he'll come out and play on occasion?" He discarded his lager and leaned in, bracing both hands either side of his plate. "As long as he knows where he stands in this relationship."

"Absolutely." I reached across the table and wrapped my hand around his. I caught his gaze and butterfly flutters filled my chest. "I gave Sammy my body, but you'll always have my heart."

He squeezed, stroking his beautiful lithe fingers along my knuckles and across the underside of my wrist. "And you know my heart only beats for you."

Funny. I'd never believed it possible—this incredible, all-encompassing love for one man. The more I discovered, the deeper he burrowed into my heart—a thought that no longer made me want to run and hide. It just made me want to know more.

I took another sip of wine. "Tell me about you and Frenemy."

"Frenemy?"

I shot him a grin. "Your recently rediscovered buddy. Damon. You know. You were once friends, then enemies. *Frenemies.*"

"O-kay."

"So, what's the story?"

"Not terribly interesting." He sighed. "Boy meets girl. Boy trusts girl with coven secrets, thinking girl will save him from immortality. Girl screws boy then passes coven secrets onto their enemies. People die. Girl disappears. Coven leader is furious. Friendship is ruined. Boy is forever marred by his stupidity."

"Fuck. That totally sucks."

"Yeah, especially for those who lost their lives."

The cut, the deep hurt and guilt were ingrained in his expression, and my heart ached with his pain. "I get why you didn't share your plan to switch the serum and save the world."

"If it's any consolation, I felt like shit for keeping it from you."

I knew that now. Knew so many things that had eluded me in the midst of my post-Richard bleeding. Not only had Gideon unlocked my emotions, he'd opened my awareness. "What happened to her?"

"Who?"

"The girl. What was her name?"

"Annaline." His beautiful lips twisted. "I don't know. We never saw her again."

"Did you love her?"

"I thought I did. But that was before I met you."

Rollicking warmth filled my chest. "But when we met, you were all about fulfilling The Prophesy. Your feelings were for your soulmate, not for *me* personally."

"At first, yes. Then I got to know you, Tiffany, the person, and mortality took on even more importance, because it meant spending the rest of my life with you."

"You say the nicest things." I pushed back my chair. Show and tell had outworn its welcome. Time now for more serious exploits.

I skirted the table and straddled his thighs. "You also do the nicest things." I rubbed my wet center against the ridge of his erection. His breath hitched, his gaze deepening to rich, forest green. "Speaking of prophesies . . . I'm thinking about the *mates of body and soul* part right now."

His palms cupped my butt, his touch so hot, so alive.

His mouth found my neck, his hot tongue laving the mark made complete by his love. My eyes fluttered closed and I shuddered, with the thought, his attention.

Yes. Our half hearts were now whole and I'd stopped questioning the verity of The Prophesy and the possibility of what other legends walked the earth outside of the books that made them renowned.

I could accept everything, endure anything, with this man by my side. Even Richard had been relegated from nuisance to nothing but an annoying blip in my past. Gideon promised a future and the nightmares of the past no longer wielded their power.

His mouth trailed down my throat, his tongue flicking between my breasts.

My breath hitched as he pulled back.

His fingers smoothed the lines either side of my mouth. "A kiss for your thoughts."

I opened my eyes. "A kiss?"

Devastating lips slid into a devastating smile. "Better than a penny."

I winked. "Depends on the kiss."

He quirked a brow. "That sounds like a challenge."

"If it walks like a duck." I grinned.

"Then a challenge, it is." He tangled his hands through my hair, twisted a curl around a finger, tugging me closer. So close, until his breath stroked my lips, his taste tantalized my tongue. "That means you go first. For a kiss."

*H*e imagined my thoughts to be good. And they were, mostly. But for undercurrents, which had faded over the past weeks.

So much had changed, so many fantasies fulfilled. Through mutual trust and honesty. Going forward, if I wanted to share the rest of my life with this man, the least I could do was share it wholly. That meant my skeletons, long burnt and buried, were about to be unearthed.

"You asked me once why I chose Louisiana as my home." I closed my eyes, bracing against the darkness and memories I could never quite shake. "Aside from the added benefit of being as far as possible from Richard, it's one place my father always said he would never, ever set foot."

His brows bounded skyward. "Your father? I thought he was dead."

A familiar burn roiled through my chest. "That would have been preferable."

"Why?" His fingers continued to tangle in my hair. Calming. Comforting. Filling me with strength to share what I'd never shared before.

"Because he killed my mother and, if I hadn't run that night, he would have killed me too."

"Fuck, Tiff. I'm so sorry." His hand left my hair to cup my jaw, his thumb lightly smoothing away the lines of my frown. "What happened?"

I shook my head. "I don't know much, and I never found out why he snapped when he did." I inhaled, fresh, soul-calming oxygen fueling my strength to continue. "My earliest childhood memories are peppered with minor bruises and cutting words. Mom threatened to leave more than once, and maybe that night she decided to follow through. Or maybe he'd had enough of playing cat and mouse. Whatever the reason, he grabbed a knife from the counter and stabbed her seventeen times."

"Hell." He looked like he wanted to hit someone. Preferably the man who'd stolen my mother and forever changed my life. "Where were you when all this happened?"

"At a party with friends. Maybe if I'd been home . . ." I

swallowed, pushing back the familiar guilt, the familiar fear. "The last time I saw my father, he was kneeling over my mother, covered head-to-toe in her blood. He looked up as I walked in, blood-red eyes cold, callous, devoid of emotion. He'd always been cruel, but that day something made me turn and run, and I never, ever looked back."

"Damn. Where is he now?" He shook his head, as if unable to believe it.

There were times I felt the same, until I recalled the metallic smack of blood hitting the back of my throat, and the burn of muscles as I ran faster and further than I'd ever run before.

"I don't know. I ran to a friend's and called the police, but before they could pick me up, I ran again. I kept running for two years, working odd jobs for cash until I'd saved enough to leave the country for good. I first moved to Washington, and you know how that worked out. The only good thing to come out of that fiasco was my citizenship. I couldn't stay, so I closed my eyes and pointed, and picked Louisiana."

His palms skimmed my shoulders to cup my biceps, massaging up and down as if to rub away the chill of my past. "Do you believe in fate?"

Eyes of ocean green dragged me deeper into his soul, and I followed, willingly. "I do now."

"Me, too." His thumb brushed my lips. "It wasn't chance that saw your finger find Louisiana."

I grinned. "It was your voodoo magic."

His brow arched, all sexy and seductive. "I thought you liked my voodoo magic."

"Just one of your many talents." I walked my fingertips

down his chest, freeing his shirt buttons from their confines. "Think I've earned that kiss?"

He waggled his brows. "With interest."

I pushed aside the fabric and smoothed my palms over hot, healthy, live skin. "Ooh, I like the sound of interest."

"One thing you should know about me and my debts." He grinned. "I always, always pay up."

"I kinda hoped you'd say that."

His lips crushed mine. Or maybe it happened in reverse. All I know is that our mouths melded, our tongues tangling in a battle for more.

I wanted more.

I pushed back his shirt the same time he struggled to rid me of my top. His mouth found my neck. "Mmm." The vibrations rocked me to my core.

He tilted his hips and the friction increased.

Fuck.

His palms found my midriff, spanning higher, caressing and cupping my breasts. I was slowly getting used to the heat of his touch. The heat of his cock as it stroked me towards mindlessness. And I wanted to feel it now. Later. Forever.

I never wanted it to stop.

39

GIDEON

Three hundred and forty-seven years had passed and my heart finally beat like it was twenty-nine.

Frost clung to the air like icicles cling to snow-kissed trees and it was a wonder to feel its bite. I raised the covers up over my shoulders and moved closer to the warm, wonderful body spooned into my front.

I felt the heated rush of blood through my veins. The heavy throb of live, pulsing flesh, still so new.

Day two of mortality.

The Prophesy had fucked up.

Was that even possible?

Not that I was questioning or complaining. I was alive. *Mortal*. It didn't matter that the antidote flowed through Tiff's blood, it could no longer harm me.

I swept my hand up over her stomach, spreading my fingers out, pressing my palm against the beat of her heart. *Two hearts made whole*. It got that part right.

The body in my arms shifted. Stretched.

A soft, contented mewl escaped her lips. I kissed the curve of her shoulder and her breath caught.

I loved that sound. All of her sounds—the happy sighs when we kissed, the contented purrs as I stroked her skin, the passionate screams as I entered her, the fervent pleas just moments before she came.

She captured my hand and inched it upwards to cup her breast. "I could get used to this."

I grinned into her neck. "That's the plan."

I teased her nipple into a taut, tantalizing bud then moved to the next. My cock nudged her ass, and she curved back, deliciously cupping it more.

She twisted, just enough to capture my mouth in a kiss. Then she spread her legs and reached between them to grasp my shaft in her hand. Slowly, fucking magically, she began to stroke. Fire flooded my balls, filling my cock, making me burn and so fucking ready.

That's when she shifted her ass, stroking the precum from my head before easing the tip through her folds and into her heat.

Nerve endings fired like Fourth of July fireworks. I slowly bucked my hips, entering and leaving her in a delicious slide that saw me fighting for breath.

"Gideon."

I ran my fingers down her tummy, through the strip of tight curls to her clit. "Tell me what you want."

She gasped. "You."

One word and my heart skipped a beat, then galloped like a horse in its first ever race. "I'm yours."

"I want to see you."

I withdrew and she turned to face me. I kissed the tip of her nose, the upward bow of her lips, the curve of her jaw.

Pushing up over her body, I pressed my cock into her flesh and lost myself in her sultry heat.

"Gideon."

My name on her lips was like birdsong on a sun-drenched summer morning. I slid deeper still, then stopped. "Tell me what you want."

"This." She splayed her hands over my hips, skimming them across my chest, up and over my shoulders. "Your body, heart and soul. Forever."

"You have them." I kissed her lips. "And now?"

Her gaze locked mine, oceans of blue dragging me in and drowning me in their hazy depths. "Love me, Gideon."

"With all my beating heart."

I slid in, balls deep, then withdrew, my gaze never once leaving hers. I watched as my love dragged her deeper into passion, her lips parted, emitting short, breathless pants as she rose then fell into climax.

Her flesh pulsed, dragging me deeper still, milking my cock into my own, mind-wrenching orgasm. She consumed me, body and soul, promising a life that spanned mortality and beyond happiness.

"Every time I think it can't get better, it does." She stroked my ego as readily as she stroked my soul.

"I aim to please." I rolled off and onto my back.

She curved into my side, one arm resting beneath her ear, the other sketching circles over my chest. "And you do that very, *very* well."

Her eyes fluttered closed, a cat-got-the-cream smile playing on her lips, her hand circling my ribs, dancing across the steady *d-dum* coming from deep within my chest. "Your heart. It's beating."

I grinned, easing her over again, sliding inside, her life and mine forever combining as one. "Only for you."

EPILOGUE

DAMON

3 months later . . .

Rip out one gray and they say two will grow back.
Not that I'd know. I hadn't sprouted a single
gray hair in the past five hundred years, and didn't expect
any to appear anytime soon.

I pushed out of the comfort of my chair and moved to the
window, to the billow of gray churning across the once blue
sky. I rolled my shoulders in an effort to iron out the kinks.
No go. The restlessness after Gideon's pairing grew greater
by the day. Not that I wasn't happy for my friend. I was.
Happy he'd found his soulmate. Happier still, he'd found
mortality and escaped The Change.

Vamps might no longer be human, but our residual
weaknesses still plague our souls. Not jealousy so much as a
twinge of "what about me?"

Half a millennium and I was still no closer to salvation.
With the responsibility of a coven to protect, and the current

shit-storm on the horizon, it seemed unlikely the situation would change anytime soon.

A moment's peace would have been welcome. But I'd learned pretty early in my leadership that wasn't how the shit rolled. It slammed against your soul and stuck fast. No sooner had we diverted the whole flu antidote issue, but we'd landed face-first in a whole dung-heap of danger.

The air shifted and I bit back a sigh. "What is it, Aaron?" I turned to find my PA shuffling his feet in my doorway.

The *swish* of his almost silent tread from halfway down the corridor had alerted me to his approach. Plus, he'd started slathering himself with that god-awful aftershave shit. Waste of time. Smelling like the sunshine rose out of your ass wouldn't attract your soulmate into your circle any faster.

Nothing would.

"Terillian wants to meet." His voice rang thick with an Australian drawl despite the fact he'd left his distant home for the States just over two centuries ago. Every time he opened his mouth, I cringed. But he was blood. And blood ran thicker than any friendship I knew. Bar one.

"Terillian can go fuck himself."

"He says we're sheltering one of his clan and he wants her back."

"Are we?"

"Not to my knowledge."

"So this is another power play?"

Aaron shrugged, the action echoing my thoughts. Terillian was a badass prick solely responsible for the rift between our two circles, and it was impossible for any rational, level-minded being to speculate on his plans. One thing I did know—the fact that he'd returned after a two hundred year sabbatical didn't bode well for either of our sides.

I didn't need Margherite's prowess at fortune-telling to know that bloodshed loomed in both our futures. What I did need, was the foresight to stop it and end Terillian's reign once and for all. Something we'd tried and failed at two centuries ago.

The memory still slumped heavy in my chest.

I sighed. "Call a meeting of the elders."

Aaron hesitated, although this time he'd breached the doorway to stand three steps shy of my desk.

I didn't even bother to hide the exasperation from my voice. "What?"

"Are you sure? Claudius is in the Maldives and you know how he'll get if we end his holiday for no reason."

No reason. What the fuck did that mean?

I'd refrained from calling on the council when the Flu A antidote threatened our mortality, our entire existence. I'd made the hard decisions, and run a successful mission with only their nod of approval from the sidelines. But this . . . this was different. It was Terillian. Akin to the devil absconding from the depths of hell, wielding his vengeance and waging terror on earth.

"I'm not sure a war is *no reason.*" I felt the descent of my fangs, the roar of a hurricane rising up from my chest. One day, he'd question me one too many times. *"Call them."*

Aaron bowed, more a nod than a full-on bob, and I turned back to the thick sheet of rain masking my view.

Things were about to get nasty for the coven, with no guarantee we'd all get out alive.

I inhaled, bracing against the window ledge, as cold as the blood that bolted through my veins.

There was one thing I hated more than the threat of The Change. *Werewolves*.

ABOUT THE AUTHOR

M L Winters is the paranormal persona of romantic suspense author, Michelle Somers. She's a bookworm from way back. An ex-Kiwi who now calls Australia home, she's a professional killer and matchmaker, a storyteller and a romantic. Words are her power and her passion. Her heroes and heroines always get their happy ever after, but she'll put them through one hell of a journey to get there.

Michelle lives in Melbourne, Australia, with her real life hero and three little heroes in the making. And her black cat, Emmie, who thinks she's a dog. Her debut novel, *Lethal in Love* won the Romance Writers of Australia's 2016 Romantic Book of the Year (RuBY) and the 2013 Valerie Parv Award.

Michelle loves hearing from her readers, so please visit her at www.michelle-somers.com

 facebook.com/MichelleSomersAuthor

twitter.com/msomerswriter

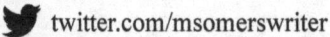 instagram.com/michellesomers00

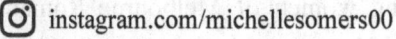 pinterest.com/michelles3268

ACKNOWLEDGEMENTS

"The further you get away from yourself, the more challenging it is. Not to be in your comfort zone is great fun."

———————

Benedict Cumberbatch hit the nail squarely on its head.

When I first started this writing journey, never once did I imagine I'd venture into dark, paranormal realms. If I'd realized the fun I'd have following the lives and loves of vampires, werewolves and magical folk, I'd have ventured much sooner!

A huge, heartfelt thank you to Fiona Miers for encouraging me out of my comfort zone. Your support, encouragement and inspiration is a truly beautiful and selfless thing.

Romance Roomies, you guys rock. Lauren Harbor, Miranda Morgan and Samara Parish, thank you for your ongoing love, support and late-night messaging. And Lauren Harbor, thank you for Safe Harbor Virtual's sock-rocking blurb.

The amazing women of Melbourne Romance Writer's Guild have guided, nurtured and supported me from the very beginning of this crazy-wonderful writing journey — I thank and love each and every one of you.

Romance Writers Australia (RWA) — your camaraderie, support and generosity of knowledge lifts writers up and gives them wings. You're an awesome group and I feel very proud to be a part of your ranks.

So many minds and helping hands made *Her Biker's Bite* the story it is today. Thank you to Rachel Bailey for your guidance and brainstorming for a tear-jerking turning point. Natasha Devereux, you came willingly to my aid when I needed NOLA knowledge. Esther Clark, your Buffy references and vampire insights made all the difference to the writing of this story. And Louisa West, thanks for the ice-breaker idea that propelled Gideon and Tiff into romance.

Thanks to my fabulous editor, Carolyn Depew, for not only editing, but for giving insight into what you can and can't do on a Harley. Appreciation to M L Tompsett for her fab job of formatting. And as always, a huge shout-out to my talented cover designer, Lana Pecherczyk.

My family — my four beautiful boys, Danny, Josh, Nathan and Gabriel. Your unwavering belief, your hugs and your praise helped me step outside my comfort zone to follow my dreams. You are my inspiration. I love you with all my heart.

Finally, to my readers, both old and new. Your thoughtful and generous reviews and words of encouragement keep me going on days when my characters won't do or go where they're supposed to.

Thank you.

COMING SOON!

HIS FORBIDDEN BITE

Forbidden lovers torn apart by betrayal...
...and an ancient prophecy that could bind them forever.

ANNALINE is a werewolf in hiding. But two centuries is long enough. Magical powers are at play, and the mystical Blood Heart stone is at risk of falling into enemy hands—an enemy hell bent on ruling werewolves and wiping out vamps. He must be stopped. That means enlisting help from the vampire she betrayed. If only Damon didn't want her dead. She's determined to find the stone and win Damon's trust, but will she ever find a way back into his heart?

Annaline will risk everything to prove her love. Even her life.

DAMON is seeking vengeance on the werewolf who betrayed him. When Annaline broke his heart and shattered his trust, she put all vampires at risk. Now he's going to end her life and forever sever the strings tying him to past mistakes. But an ancient prophecy forces them together in a race against time, and a common enemy. Damon fights their sizzling attraction, but when Annaline saves his life, his icy fury thaws. He's torn. Because the one woman he shouldn't love still holds his heart... and the key to saving his soul.

HIS FORBIDDEN BITE is a steamy, save the world romance of forbidden love between a sexy vampire and his sassy werewolf counterpart. This book marks the second in my STEAMY BITES series, and it's full of sizzle and suspense. Make sure you read with the aircon on high!